I never imagined that pretending to be married to Connor McKay would lead to real-life wedded bliss and motherhood. From the first moment I held baby Sarah in my arms I knew it was my destiny to be her mother and Connor's wife.

I've always wanted a husband and a family of my own to love. Who would have thought that a little pink bundle with ten tiny fingers and ten chubby toes would lead Connor and me to discover the love of a lifetime?

The three of us may not have gotten together in the most conventional way, but it is undeniable that we belong together.

1. ALABAMA
Late Bloomer—Peg Sutherland
2. ALASKA
Casey's Flyboy—Vivian Leiber
3. ARIZONA
Second Wife—Stephanie James
4. ARKANSAS
Bittersweet Sacrifice—Bay Matthews
5. CALIFORNIA
Hunter's Way—Justine Davis
6. COLORADO
Rafferty's Choice—Dallas Schulze
7. CONNECTICUT
Special Delivery—Judith Arnold
8. DELAWARE
Taking Love in Stride—Donna Clayton
9. FLORIDA
Marriage by the Book—Joan Johnston
10. GEORGIA
Baby, It's You—Celeste Hamilton
11. HAWAII
Daddy's Girl—Barbara Bretton
12. IDAHO
One of the Family—Kristine Rolofson
13. ILLINOIS
Above Suspicion—Andrea Edwards
14. INDIANA
Intrusive Man—Lass Small
15. IOWA
Count Your Blessings—Kathy Clark
16. KANSAS
Patchwork Family—Carla Cassidy
17. KENTUCKY
Heart's Journey—Cathy Gillen Thacker
18. LOUISIANA
Crazy Like a Fox—Anne Stuart
19. MAINE
Fantasies and Memories—Muriel Jensen
20. MARYLAND
Minor Miracles—Rebecca Flanders
21. MASSACHUSETTS
Only the Nanny Knows for Sure—Phyllis Halldorson
22. MICHIGAN
The Proper Miss Porter—Ruth Langan
23. MINNESOTA
Emily's House—Nikki Benjamin
24. MISSISSIPPI
Beloved Stranger—Peggy Webb
25. MISSOURI
Head Over Heels—Leigh Roberts

26. MONTANA
Renegade Son—Lisa Jackson
27. NEBRASKA
Abracadabra—Peg Sutherland
28. NEVADA
Chances—Janice Kaiser
29. NEW HAMPSHIRE
Racing with the Moon—Muriel Jensen
30. NEW JERSEY
Romeo in the Rain—Kasey Michaels
31. NEW MEXICO
Desperate Measures—Paula Detmer Riggs
32. NEW YORK
Honorable Intentions—Judith McWilliams
33. NORTH CAROLINA
Twice in a Lifetime—BJ James
34. NORTH DAKOTA
Letters of Love—Judy Kaye
35. OHIO
One to One—Marisa Carroll
36. OKLAHOMA
Last Chance Cafe—Curtiss Ann Matlock
37. OREGON
Home Fires—Candace Schuler
38. PENNSYLVANIA
Thorne's Wife—Joan Hohl
39. RHODE ISLAND
Somebody's Hero—Kristine Rolofson
40. SOUTH CAROLINA
The Sea at Dawn—Laurie Paige
41. SOUTH DAKOTA
Night Light—Jennifer Greene
42. TENNESSEE
Somebody's Baby—Marilyn Pappano
43. TEXAS
The Heart's Yearning—Ginna Gray
44. UTAH
Wild Streak—Pat Tracy
45. VERMONT
MacKenzie's Baby—Anne McAllister
46. VIRGINIA
First Things Last—Dixie Browning
47. WASHINGTON
Belonging—Sandra James
48. WEST VIRGINIA
The Baby Track—Barbara Boswell
49. WISCONSIN
Fly Away—Pamela Browning
50. WYOMING
The Last Good Man Alive—Myrna Temte

Please address questions and book requests to: Silhouette Reader Service
U.S.: 3010 Walden Ave., P.O. Box 1325, Buffalo, NY 14269
Canadian: P.O. Box 609, Fort Erie, Ont. L2A 5X3

WEST VIRGINIA

BARBARA BOSWELL

The Baby Track

Silhouette Books

Published by Silhouette Books
America's Publisher of Contemporary Romance

SILHOUETTE BOOKS
300 East 42nd St.,
New York, N.Y. 10017

ISBN 0-373-47198-X

THE BABY TRACK

Copyright © 1991 by Barbara Boswell

Printed in U.S.A.

Dear Reader,

I was delighted to learn that *The Baby Track* had been selected for Silhouette Books' BORN IN THE USA series. I've always enjoyed reading stories with babies in them, and writing one proved to be fun and challenging. A baby in a romance novel can bring a couple closer, but putting the needs of an infant before their own also can provide a conflict between the hero and heroine—especially when they don't know each other very well. Courtney and Connor in *The Baby Track* are strangers who become parents even before they are lovers. Not the usual sequence of events, but happily it works for them.

The story is set in the fictitious town of Shadyside Falls in the very real state of West Virginia. Although I'm a native Pennsylvanian, I've always considered West Virginia my "second home state." My sister Monica and her husband and their four children live in Charleston, the state capital, which I visit several times a year. My daughter and her husband are also graduates of WVU in Morgantown, a place with many happy memories for all of us. At the risk of sounding like a member of the chamber of commerce, I encourage everybody to visit West Virginia. To quote that John Denver song—which was also the state motto for a while—the place is "Almost Heaven," with its mountains, lakes, and white water for outdoor activities, the warm and friendly people who live there, and its interesting history.

Barbara Boswell

One

"Come back!" The outraged secretary chased Connor McKay through the narrow corridor. "Ms. Carey is in conference." The woman's voice rose with indignation. "She is not to be disturbed under any circumstances!"

Connor merely ignored her and proceeded along the hall until he came to a door bearing the nameplate of Courtney Carey. He stopped in front of it.

"Sir, you cannot see Ms. Carey without an appointment," the secretary snapped as he fastened his hand around the doorknob. She caught up to him and reached out her arm, as if to physically restrain him.

Connor decided he admired her tenacious dedication to her boss's schedule. It was a good quality for a staff member to have, and he'd keep it in mind should he ever acquire a staff to command.

"You can't go in there!" the woman reiterated sternly.

Connor flashed a grin. "Watch me." He turned the knob, pushed open the door and stepped into the office.

Courtney Carey was sitting at her desk, unwrapping a foot-long cheesesteak. Her head jerked up as the door opened, and she gaped as a tall, muscular man, somewhere in his mid-thirties and wearing jeans and a leather bomber jacket, strode into her office. She quickly adjusted her gaping jaw, but continued to study the man as he crossed the office to stand in front of her desk. He was not the usual sort of visitor here, neither an expensively tailored corporate sponsor type nor one of the funky artistic individuals who frequented the offices of the National Public Broadcasting Network.

This man could not be so neatly categorized. He was tanned and rugged and his sandy brown hair was worn too long for a businessman but too short for an artist. His clothing—jeans, jacket, blue oxford-cloth shirt and high-top canvas shoes—was a mixture of the traditional and the unconventional. He was tall, well over six feet, and towered above her secretary, Mimi Ditmar, who had bustled in, red-faced and irate, after him.

"Courtney, I'm so sorry," Mimi said, casting a glare at the office intruder. "I tried to keep this—person—out, but he pushed his way inside."

"Miss Carey is in conference, hmm?" Connor interrupted, glancing pointedly around the empty office. He focused his gaze directly on Courtney, who was still clutching her sandwich. She quickly shoved it back into the paper bag.

"Ms. Carey is obviously not in conference," snapped Mimi. "She is having her lunch break, as you can very well see."

Connor shrugged. "I've always heard how creative you folks here at NPB are. I thought maybe she was conferring with the sandwich instead of eating it. An original twist on a mundane activity, perhaps?"

Courtney bit back the retort that instantly sprang to mind. She didn't know who this man was; it wouldn't do to insult him...just yet. "We creative types have to eat, too," she said, mildly enough. Only her flashing dark eyes belied her unruffled demeanor.

"But you find it beneath your dignity to admit to such primitive urges so you instruct your guard dog to say you're in conference instead of having lunch." Connor's smile was as challenging as his words, as baiting as his tone.

Mimi gasped with offended disapproval.

"Mrs. Ditmar isn't anyone's guard dog." Courtney rose to her feet. "You owe her an apology. And then I want you to leave my office immediately." Now was definitely the time to insult him, whoever he may be.

"You're throwing me out?" Connor walked to the window, then turned around to face both women. He was clearly unmoved by the chastisement; nor did he seem even slightly insulted. "You don't even know who I am. What if I'm an eccentric billionaire who's come with a seven-figure check to donate to National Public Broadcasting, a sum so big it'll catapult your struggling new network out of the red and into the heady zones of profit?"

Courtney folded her arms in front of her chest. "Somehow I doubt that. Your appearance and your behavior places you firmly in the company of Philistines R Us. Kindly leave now or I'll be forced to call security and have you removed."

"Speech by phrase-o-matic." Connor arched his dark brows. "Maybe you aren't so creative after all, Miss Carey."

"I'm calling security this instant!" Mimi announced, reaching for the phone on Courtney's desk.

"If security is that seventy-five-year-old guy dozing in the lounge chair by the elevator, I'd advise you not to bother," said Connor. "He's not going to remove me unless I agree to be removed. And that won't be until after I've talked with Miss Carey. Privately," he added succinctly, with a dismissive glance at Mimi Ditmar.

"It's all right, Mimi. I'll talk with him," Courtney interjected before her secretary could object. "Go on back to your desk."

She was not ceding defeat, Courtney assured herself, she was simply facing reality. The man had no intention of leaving, and the sooner she talked to him, the sooner he would go away.

"Sensible course of action, Miss Carey," said Connor. "I promise not to take up too much of your valuable time. You'll be back in conference with your sandwich quite soon."

Her lips tight with disapproval, Mimi left the office, pulling the door closed behind her with unrestrained force.

"Did I say she was a guard dog?" Connor grinned. "Let me amend that to lady dragon."

"Mimi is very dedicated and protective of my time," Courtney told him shortly. She sat back down in her chair, a strategic move designed to command control of this meeting that she'd been forced to accept. It was important to regain the lost initiative. "What do you want, Mr.—" she paused, waiting for him to supply his name.

"McKay. Connor McKay." He knew something about strategic moves himself and leaned against the corner of her desk, propping his right thigh on the edge of it. He stared down at the young woman sitting in the desk chair only a few feet away from him.

She was not at all what he'd been expecting. Although he'd never set foot in the NPB offices until today, he had assumed that anyone who worked for the fledgling network, with its proud pledge of "Profound, Innovative and Cogitative Programming," must be the stereotypical intellectual bluestocking. Cerebral and officious, emanating an unmistakable air of superiority; hair styled in a no-nonsense bowl cut, feet encased in sensible oxfords. Unattractive and proud of it. Mimi Ditmar had perfectly fit his profile.

Courtney Carey did not. In any setting, she would draw a second—third, fourth, fifth!—glance. When she had been standing, he'd gauged her height to be slightly above average, about five-foot-five, and her figure was way above average. Though she wore an uninspiring starched white blouse with a high collar and long sleeves, it could not conceal the lush curves of her breasts beneath it. Her pencil-slim forest-green skirt was as plain as her blouse but adeptly displayed her small waist, flat stomach and the sweet, sexy flare of her hips.

She had thick, dark hair that fell to her shoulders, in a soft, glossy mane. Her face was equally arresting. Enormous wide-set brown eyes that were alert and intelligent and as dark and soft as velvet. High cheekbones and a firm little chin. And her mouth... A sudden and wholly unexpected surge of heat suffused his body. Her mouth was enticing, alluring, the beautiful line of her lips wide and sensually shaped. Connor found himself swallowing hard.

Courtney was fully aware of his masculine surveillance, of course. She watched his sea-green eyes slide over her and forced herself to remain still in her seat while keeping her expression carefully impassive. Surprisingly it was an effort to do so. She felt...strange.

Normally such a blatant male once-over disgusted her. If she were in a particularly good mood and the overlooker was absurdly, comically obvious about it, she occasionally found it amusing. She couldn't understand why this man's long, illicit gaze, designed to inspect, appraise and assess her, was not producing her usual hostile or condescending responses.

But it wasn't. She felt something else entirely, a peculiar feeling that she didn't recognize and couldn't identify. That worried her. The last thing she wanted was for some stranger to come barging into her neatly planned life, evoking feelings she didn't want and couldn't control.

A protective, defensive surge of anger ribboned through her. Courtney gave her head a slight shake, as if to clear away all unmanageable thoughts, and fixed her lips into a taut smile.

"Well, Mr. McKay, since you've insisted upon this meeting, I suggest you state your business."

She was pleased by the sound of her voice, firm and cool and strictly no-nonsense. Such a well-modulated, controlled voice proved that she was unaffected by the hard-edged and handsome features of his face, that she was equally unmoved by his densely muscled body.

Still, she pushed her chair back, angling away from him. He was entirely too close in his current position.

"My business," Connor drawled, deliberately leaning forward. His unnerving momentary loss of composure had passed and he was back in control again. And thoroughly enjoying the fact that his nearness was making Miss Courtney Carey antsy enough to wobble on two feet of her chair. He was sure that she normally kept all four feet of the chair firmly on the ground.

"Suppose I were to tell you that you're my business, Courtney." He grinned as her mouth tightened in disapproval at his unsolicited familiarity.

She stood up and moved swiftly away from him. "Is this a joke?" Her big dark eyes were fiery. "Did someone hire you to—to—" she paused, waiting for him to supply an answer.

He didn't. "Hire me to do what?" he asked interestedly.

A crimson flush stained her cheeks. "To come here and—"

"And?" Connor prodded. "Don't keep me in suspense, Courtney."

The gleam in his eyes was paradoxically both taunting and rakishly inviting. Courtney felt her pulse begin to race. She'd never seen eyes that particular color before, a dark ocean-green. And at this moment, they looked as wild and turbulent as a stormy sea.

"You know very well," she said brusquely, willing herself to calm down. "You were hired to come to my office and—and shake me up." Embarrassed, she lowered her voice and averted her gaze.

"You mean there's a market for that?" Connor asked incredulously.

He was laughing. At her, Courtney was certain. She clenched her jaw tightly.

"No kidding?" Connor persisted. "Do people actually hire people to go into offices and—"

"Read pornographic poems or telegrams," Courtney cut in crossly, "or put on music and strip or something similarly obnoxious. You needn't sound so surprised and ingenuous, Mr. McKay. You can't tell me that you've never heard of that kind of—of novelty service."

"Is that what they're calling it these days?" Connor's voice was full of laughter. "You creative intellectuals really are imaginative. Sorry, I don't have any erotic poems with me. Do you want me to improvise? Here goes... There once was a girl named Fay, who was one helluva—" he paused. "Nah, I'll skip the poetry and take it all off instead. If you'll hum a few bars of 'The Stripper,' please?"

He pulled off his jacket and tossed it over a chair. Courtney watched, wide-eyed, as his fingers moved to the top button of his shirt. "Stop!" she exclaimed.

Thankfully he did. "So who do you think hired me to come into your office, Miss Carey?" he drawled.

Courtney seethed. "Does the name Jarrell Harcourt mean anything to you?"

"No. Should it?"

"Be fair, Mr. McKay. If Jarrell hired you, you should at least be honest and own up to it." Courtney frowned. "She's the only one I can think of who would want to—" She took a deep breath and did not finish.

"Embarrass you?" Connor suggested helpfully.

Unfortunately he was right on target, but Courtney

wasn't about to admit that to him. She stared stonily into space, saying nothing.

Connor was undeterred by her silence. "So you believe that one of your friends would hire someone to bust into your office for the sole purpose of humiliating you? Some friend! I know you upper-class, pretentious snobs have your own odd customs, but—"

"I am not an upper-class, pretentious snob," Courtney inserted testily.

"But I'll take odds that Jarrell Harcourt is. Her name is a dead giveaway." Connor moved off the desk and took a step toward her. She automatically took a step backward. "So how come this Harcourt bitch has it in for you?"

"You shouldn't call her that," Courtney protested.

Too weakly, she realized, for Connor immediately came back with: "Why not? She must be one if she hires professionals to harass, embarrass and otherwise unnerve her alleged friends."

"How did we get into this ridiculous conversation, anyway?" Courtney sighed impatiently. "This whole thing has gone far enough, Mr. McKay. I demand that you—"

"Does Mimi know who Jarrell Harcourt is? Maybe I'll go ask her since you won't tell me." Connor headed for the door.

"Oh, for heaven's sake!" Courtney grated. "Jarrell Harcourt is the sister of a man I've dated. Now, will you *please*—"

"And she doesn't like you or the fact that you date her brother," Connor surmised. "Why not?"

Courtney knew she shouldn't answer him. She should completely ignore him before he took any sort of response at all for encouragement. The last thing this brash barbarian needed was encouragement of any kind. Having reached that conclusion, she was stunned to hear herself snap, "Since you're so quick on the uptake I'm surprised you haven't figured it out for yourself."

"Hmm. Let me scope it out." He glanced from her to the paper bag and can of soda pop on her desk. "I do have a few clues. For instance, wouldn't a stuck-up snob eat something equally insufferable? Something like pâté and watercress on toast points from some upscale, trendy place? And of course, the beverage of choice wouldn't be good old all-American cola like you have here, it would have to be the latest in designer spring water or something similarly snotty."

He picked up the oily bag and read the name printed on it. "Herman's Deli. I know the place. It's a hole-in-the-wall in a downscale, decidedly nontrendy area of the city, but they deliver anywhere. Even here, it seems."

Connor frowned thoughtfully. "So I'm going to go out on a limb and guess that the reason why the Harcourt broad doesn't like you dating her brother is because she doesn't approve of you. Your patronage of Herman's Deli and those big gypsy eyes of yours give you away, Courtney Carey. You might be one of NPB's cerebral highbrows, but you're not a rich, upper-class snob whose birth certificate entitles you to travel in the Harcourts' blue-blooded circles." He arched his dark, thick brows and smiled sardonically. "Though you damn well wish you were."

He'd zeroed in with unerring accuracy on the reason for Jarrell Harcourt's disapproval of her, but he was way off the mark otherwise. "I do *not* want to be a rich snob, and I resent your accusation as much as I resent Jarrell Harcourt's suspicions that I'm out to snare her defenseless brother.'' Courtney shot him a look of pure dislike. "I've humored you long enough, *Connor*.'' She scornfully emphasized his first name to underscore her contempt for his unwarranted familiarity. "Get out of my office. Right now.''

Instead of leaving, he dropped into her desk chair. "You cut me to the quick, honey. I don't mind you ordering me out of your office, but dropping the respectful Mr. McKay for *Connor* was a low blow.'' He shook his head. "It's going to take me a long time to recover from that one.''

Courtney flushed. She was humiliated. And furious. And frustrated. She was getting nowhere with this disrespectful smart aleck, while he was having a field day mocking her. What was even worse was the uneasy notion that she was ably assisting him in making a fool of her.

"Who are you?'' she ground out, clenching her fingers into fists. Her palms were itching with the urge to slap that handsome face of his, to wipe off the mocking smile. It was a totally uncharacteristic impulse for her, for she loathed violence of any sort. Why, every holiday season she picketed the office of a toy store chain protesting their sale of war toys and martial arts items!

She was committed to settling disputes with words, but at this moment, she very much wanted to smack the sarcastic smile off Connor McKay's face. Horrified, Courtney put her hands behind her back.

"I already told you my name,'' Connor said, shrugging dismissively, seemingly unaware of her inner turmoil.

Or if he were aware, it didn't bother him in the least. Her anger rose with alarming force. "Then *what* are you?"

"I'm something of a private investigator," he replied nonchalantly.

Courtney stared at him, momentarily agog. "You mean, like a policeman?"

"No, Gypsy. Nothing at all like a policeman."

"Stop being so oblique. And don't call me Gypsy."

"You look like a gypsy girl. Sultry, sexy. Hot dark eyes."

"You're the one with the hot eyes," she snapped. "Don't think I'm not aware of the way you've been looking at me, stripping me naked—" She abruptly broke off, horrified with her admission. *What on earth was the matter with her?* She never blurted out her thoughts, had never once had an embarrassing slip of the tongue. Until now, in the infuriating, wicked presence of Connor McKay.

"I plead guilty to stripping you with my eyes," Connor admitted with a cool, sexy smile. "I wouldn't mind doing it with my hands, either, Gypsy. But imagine you noticing and then commenting on it! I think I'm beginning to see why Jarrell doesn't approve of you as an aspiring Harcourt."

Courtney, heralded by everybody who knew her for never losing her temper, finally lost it. She grabbed the nearest hurlable object, a large thick book on Celtic legends that had been the basis for a critically acclaimed television program last fall on NPB. Unfortunately it had suffered the usual NPB curse of dismal ratings. She drew back her arm to throw.

"As I said—hot eyes, hot-blooded." Connor's sea-green eyes gleamed. "Go ahead, throw it, baby.

That'll give me cause to come after you. Like this.''
He sprang from the chair, as swift and lithe as a leopard.

Courtney scarcely had time to blink before he was standing directly in front of her.

"And then I'll retaliate. Like this." His big hands cupped her shoulders and he pulled her against him with one deft movement.

She was so shocked that the book fell from her suddenly nerveless fingers. It landed on the carpet with a thud. Just as quickly and unexpectedly as he'd grabbed her, Connor released her. He bent down and picked up the book, then set it carefully on the top of the desk.

"But since you didn't throw the book, after all, I have no reason to retaliate, do I, Courtney?" His voice was low and husky.

They were still standing close together, and warmth pooled deep in his groin as he stared down at her, taking thorough inventory of her—her big brown eyes, that gorgeous mouth, her breasts, her slender, well-shaped legs in the sheer, cream-tinted nylons. Her dark green leather shoes were as dainty and as sexy as her small, slim feet. He inhaled the clean, fresh scent of her hair and had to restrain himself from reaching out to stroke it.

This little game was beginning to get out of hand, he realized with a start. Playing with the deceptively prim Miss Carey was too arousing, and entirely too engaging. His efficient bachelor alarm sounded. An arousing, engaging woman led to involvement, involvement inevitably meant demands and promises that swiftly escalated into commitment. He wanted none of it, not any of it.

He had let her go because he'd been astonished by how badly he wanted to keep her in his arms, but he couldn't seem to tear his eyes away from her. Another danger signal.

Courtney's heart began to thud. His gaze burned her, hot as fire, and she backed away from him. She could still feel the imprint of his warm, strong hands on her shoulders, her breasts were tingling from that momentary collision with the hard muscular wall of his chest. He was too big, too close, too intimidatingly male, and she felt scared and off balance. And furious that he could affect her in such an elemental, primitive way.

"Mr. McKay—" she began tightly.

"You are all shook up, aren't you?" Connor schooled his features into a coolly amused mask. He was relieved that she did not know how very far from cool he really was.

"If your nemesis Jarrell Harcourt actually had hired me, I definitely would've earned my salary." He laughed a pleased-with-himself laugh that set her teeth on edge.

Oh, she really did not like this man! "You've taken up enough of my time," Courtney fairly snarled. "If you don't get out immediately, I'll—"

"You'll what? Calling security and throwing a book at me have already been ruled out. Exactly what are your other options, Gypsy?" He should stop this at once, Connor reprimanded himself. A few more sparks and the electricity crackling between them would blow a fuse. But he couldn't seem to stop baiting her.

"Don't call me Gypsy! And *this* is my other option," she added dramatically, storming out of the office and slamming the door behind her. Her knees were shaking and her heartbeat thundered in her head.

She was halfway down the hall before she admitted the true reason why she had removed herself from her own office. If she hadn't left, she would've done something very physical—to him. The urge to run at him like a battering ram had been almost overwhelming. And if she had...

It didn't take much imagination to visualize herself crashing into him, and Courtney had always had a very active imagination. She carried the scenario further in her mind. He would catch her, wrapping his arms around her to brace himself against the furious thrust of her. And then he would look down at her with those hot, hungry green eyes of his. And she would—

"Courtney, what's going on? Where is that intrusive pest?"

Courtney started violently as she came face-to-face with Mimi Ditmar. "I—um—left him in my office," she said weakly.

"What does he want?" asked Mimi. "Is he selling something?"

It occurred to Courtney that she had no idea what Connor McKay really wanted or why he'd come to her office. They had kept getting sidetracked from that little issue. Her cheeks pinked. She had behaved atrociously, she reproved herself, like a headstrong, impulsive adolescent instead of the jack-of-all-trades—writer, editor and programming/production assistant—that she was. Working in public television, particularly for a new network, meant doing a little, sometimes a lot, of everything.

Connor McKay, a salesman? That hadn't even occurred to her. "I came out here to get—" Courtney stared at Mimi's desk, saw the stack of papers and improvised "—a copy of the transcript of our show on the early days of the American cinema." She snatched a copy from the top of the pile.

"He's interested in the early days of American cinema?" Mimi appeared stunned. "What is he, a filmmaker? One of those wild nonconformist types from Hollywood?"

There had never actually been a wild nonconformist type from Hollywood in the Washington, D.C., office of NPB, but Courtney supposed that Connor McKay might be Mimi's idea of one. She almost smiled.

But she didn't. She had left a stranger in her office while she'd run off like a high-strung schoolgirl, she reminded herself. A sobering thought, indeed.

"I don't know what to make of him, Mimi," she said frankly. She did know that he'd had a powerful impact on her, that she had never met another man who affected her so viscerally, so physically. And that made him dangerous, indeed.

He was also still in her office and she had no other choice but to return and deal with him. Courtney squared her shoulders and headed back down the corridor toward her office, the transcript in her hand.

It would be just her luck if Connor McKay turned out to be who he had claimed he was when he'd first entered her office—an eccentric billionaire with a seven-figure check to donate to National Public Broadcasting, a sum that would catapult the struggling three-year-old network out of the red and into the heady zones of profit.

Courtney found herself half believing it by the time she'd reached her office. She opened the door and stepped inside.

Two

He was sitting behind her desk, eating her cheese-steak.

"It's great." Connor held up the other, untouched half of the sandwich. "Have some."

Courtney reached an irrevocable conclusion. "Who-ever— and whatever—you are, you are definitely *not* an eccentric billionaire with a generous donation for the network."

He laughed. "Don't tell me you actually thought I was? Say, would you like to buy some oceanfront property in Nebraska?"

She walked over to her desk and snatched the other half of her cheesesteak. "I don't recall asking you to join me for lunch. And I certainly didn't invite you to *eat* my lunch."

"You couldn't eat the whole thing by yourself. This is a big sandwich for such a little girl."

Courtney rolled her eyes heavenward. "I'm twenty-five years old, I'm self-supporting and a taxpayer. What I am *not* is a little girl."

"Twenty-five, huh? You look younger."

"If that's a compliment, thank you. If it's an insult, consider it ignored." She sat down on the only other chair in her small office, which was placed alongside her desk. "And the reason why I ordered the full-sized cheesesteak is precisely because I *can* eat the whole thing myself. I'm starving. I had no breakfast this morning and very little dinner last night." She took a generous bite of the sandwich. What was the point of standing on ceremony with this office-crashing lunch-napper?

"Harcourt was too stingy to spring for dinner, wore you out in bed and then cheaped-out on breakfast, too, huh?"

Her head jerked up and her eyes collided with his. To her everlasting consternation, she blushed. "That is none of your business, Mr. McKay."

"This Harcourt guy sounds like a major pain, Gypsy. He's cheap, he has a sister who doesn't like you. Is he really worth your time?"

"I refuse to discuss Emery Harcourt with—"

"*Emery?* You've got to be kidding. His name is Emery Harcourt? Honey, he'd better be dynamite in the sack to make up for that."

Courtney tossed down her sandwich and jumped to her feet. "He is not dynamite in the sack! And I—"

"I'm sorry to hear that," Connor cut in gleefully. "But no sorrier than you, I'm sure. So, you're after him strictly for his money, hmm?"

"You're deliberately misinterpreting everything I say!" Courtney accused. Part of her acknowledged that she was overreacting to his teasing and that he was reveling in her heated responses, but she promptly absolved herself. The man frustrated her beyond endurance!

Connor finished his half of the sandwich and took a long swallow from the can of cola. "What's to misinterpret, Courtney? It all seems pretty clear-cut to me. You're an ambitious, social-climbing gold digger who doesn't mind putting up with cheap, impotent Emery Harcourt because—"

"He is not impotent! That is, even if he is, I wouldn't know because I've never slept with him." She glowered forbiddingly, trying to stem the insidious blush suffusing her cheeks. She could not remember ever being quite this mortified. "I've known him for several years and—"

"*Years?*" Connor's voice rose on an incredulous squeak. "You've been going with this guy for *years* and you've never slept with him?"

For the first time since he'd barged into her office, he appeared totally nonplussed. Which just illustrated that, in addition to all his other sins, Connor McKay was also one of those appalling fast and demanding rogues who expected women to hop into bed with him upon command—undoubtedly on the first date!

He also jumped to conclusions—the wrong ones. She'd been about to explain that her relationship with Emery had always been platonic, from their first meeting here at the NPB offices, where he'd come to meet with members of the board. There was no chemistry between them, but they enjoyed each other's company and occasionally served as each other's escorts when one was needed for certain occasions. Lately she'd been seeing quite a bit of Emery; the woman he had hoped to marry had found someone else and he was taking the breakup hard. Courtney was providing the undemanding company and support he needed, but his dreadful sister Jarrell had completely misinterpreted the rela- tionship. And now, so had Connor McKay.

Courtney decided that she owned him no explanations; in fact, he didn't deserve one! She scowled. "I wouldn't expect you to understand the sensitivity and tact of a gentleman like Emery Harcourt," she said with a haughty sniff.

"The guy must have a hormone deficiency if he hasn't tried to make it with you," Connor said flatly. "You're a knockout, Gypsy. A woman as sexy as you makes a man's blood run hot by just looking at you."

Courtney opened her mouth to speak, then abruptly closed it. She didn't know how to reply. Sexy, her? A knockout? No man had ever given her such a fulsome compliment. She suspected that she ought to be annoyed because it was an undeniably sexist remark; instead, a peculiar, slow warmth stole through her.

"Well." Courtney stared at the floor. She self-consciously smoothed her hair with her hand in a nervous gesture that made him smile. "You shouldn't talk to me that way," she murmured at last.

"You're right, I shouldn't. We could both end up in big trouble. You're determined to pursue a sterile but undoubtedly meaningful relationship with the bloodless Emery Harcourt, and I'm determined to avoid anything remotely resembling a meaningful relationship. Let's talk about something else. Wilson Nollier, for instance."

Courtney went very still. "Wilson Nollier?" she repeated carefully. "The attorney?"

"There are those who would call him something

else. Like a baby broker." Connor shrugged. "A broker puts together buyers and sellers and takes a cut of the action. That seems to be what Nollier is doing, running a lucrative business where babies are bought and sold like commodities."

Courtney's eyes widened. "I've been researching the topic of adoption for a program I'm hoping will air on NPB. I've talked to a number of couples who have used Wilson Nollier to handle their adoptions and—"

"I know," Connor injected. "I got your name from all of them. And I'm here to ask you to bug off. Please," he added as an apparent afterthought. "You're encroaching on my territory. Too many questions are being asked, and people are getting nervous and clamming up. You're wrecking my investigation, Gypsy."

"Investigation?" she repeated, staring thoughtfully at him. He'd already said he wasn't a policeman. "Are you a reporter?"

"Not exactly. I earn my living collecting facts, but I don't write the stories that use them." It was a perfect job for the uninvolved, uncommitted life-style he'd chosen for himself. Get the facts and turn them over to someone else, then move on to something else. Crafting a story, a report, took too much time; there was too much involvement with the subject at hand. He wanted no ties—to anything.

Courtney was frowning. "What kind of a job is that?" she demanded. As one who threw herself heart and soul into a project, she recognized a shirker. "You investigate stories but don't report them? Are you some sort of hired gun? The kind who tracks unfaithful spouses to sleazy hotels and takes pictures?'' She didn't bother to conceal her disapproval.

Connor laughed. ''That's PD work, honey. Not my line. The results of my investigations are used in stories, not divorce court. I like investigating—the thrill of the chase, gathering the pieces of the puzzle. So I turn in the facts and the desk jockeys in the office put them together for the magazine and the show.''

''What magazine and what show?''

''*Insight* magazine. And syndicated television's *Inside Copy.* I work for both. In fact, I sort of invented the job of full-time fact finder,'' Connor admitted jauntily. ''But it's a surprisingly lucrative field. I also occasionally freelance for the other quasi-news TV shows. Ever tune in?''

''No,'' Courtney said bluntly. ''I don't read *Insight,* either, unless I have a long wait in the dentist's office or supermarket checkout line.''

Insight was a slick, gossipy magazine featuring pictures and stories about celebrities from every walk of life, as well as average citizens whose lives had taken a newsworthy turn, sometimes inspiring, usually ghoulish, but always informative or entertaining, according to *Insight*'s massive marketing campaign. Since bursting onto the publication scene five years ago in a carefully orchestrated media blitz, *Insight*'s circulation had steadily increased until it had become a worthy rival of its popular forerunners.

On its three-color logo, *Insight* proudly described itself as ''infotainment,'' a word combining information and entertainment that Courtney considered gaggingly cutesy. *Inside Copy,* the magazine's TV equivalent, was ''infotainment,'' too.

''Let me guess—you consider infotainment beneath

your lofty public broadcasting values," Connor
taunted.

Courtney grimaced. Ugh! He'd actually used the re-
pulsive word in conversation. "*Insight* is a step above
the sleazy supermarket tabloids," she conceded. "*Inside Copy* is a television tabloid. Enough said."

"Why hold a grudge against them, Gyps? *Insight*
and *Copy* fans don't begrudge you NPB's offerings
for eggheads. There's room in the marketplace for
both."

"Unfortunately there isn't room for both," Courtney said flatly. "NPB's educational magazine was
forced to cease production because of decreasing circulation. And our network scrimps along on a shoe-
string budget while trying to offer television programs
that are culturally edifying and enlightening while
shows like *Inside Copy* earn profits by appealing
to—"

"Save it for the next NPB fund-raiser, Courtney.
The truth is that *Insight* is rolling in dough because it
delivers what the public wants to a wide audience. The
same principle applies to television. *Insight* and *Inside
Copy* are fun, a mindless escape. Your ponderous doc-
umentaries on subjects like collective farming in Al-
bania and nature studies of obscure animals are downright tedious."

"We'll have to agree to disagree on that, won't
we?" she retorted. "But I won't agree to giving up
my research on adoption. I started out as a reporter
here at the station, but for the past year I've been
doing editing, producing and programming, a bit of
everything, actually. This is a story I wanted to report
and write myself, and my boss gave me the go-ahead.
I'm doing just that—going ahead with it, despite your

investigation or fact-finding or whatever it is you call what you do for *Insight* and *Inside Copy*.''

Connor heaved an impatient sigh. "Can we at least work out some kind of compromise? You do your program on foreign adoptions and adoptions handled through the licensed state agencies. *Insight* will do the story on private adoptions, including Wilson Nollier's racket, of course.''

She shook her head. "Since Nollier seems to have crossed the line from the gray market to black market adoptions, he belongs in NPB's documentary.''

"Courtney, if both of us go after Nollier, he'll suspect something. I told you that I've already interviewed the same adoptive parents you have. They mentioned your name and the program you planned to do for NPB. They were already having second thoughts about talking to either of us. There's a chance one of them might open up to one of us, but never to both.''

"And you think that one ought to be you, not me,'' Courtney said coolly.

"That's right. Let's face facts, honey. More people are going to read *Insight* or watch *Inside Copy* than tune into your well-meaning documentary on NPB. And I want to alert the public to Nollier's racket.''

He definitely had a point there, especially considering NPB's unhappy ratings in the Neilsen's. But give up the story? Courtney shook her head. "NPB has a number of powerful benefactors,'' she argued. "They could use their pull and their prestige to put a stop to Nollier if they were allied to the program—which they would be if it aired on NPB.''

It was a standoff. They stood facing each other, each waiting for the other's next move.

"We're not getting anywhere on this," Connor growled. "I'm not used to being stonewalled, baby."

"Don't call me baby," she snapped. "I'm not a casual pickup. And I'm not stonewalling you, either." She somehow instinctively knew that what he wasn't used to was having a woman not give in to his wishes, whatever they happened to be. The perception annoyed her more than it should have.

The silence stretched between them. At last, Connor reached inside his jacket and pulled out a packet, which he tossed onto the desk. "That's my report on Nollier. Read it and you'll see why this guy has got to be put out of business as soon as possible."

He frowned. The facts in his report haunted him; he couldn't seem to blithely shake them off. "I've interviewed both adoptive parents and birth mothers who used Nollier to handle the adoptions. A direct conflict of interest there, but Nollier's only interest is in the fat fee he collects when the baby is handed over."

"I agree that Wilson Nollier's racket has to end." Courtney looked troubled. "But it's been impossible for me to find anyone willing to talk on the record about him, so I can't use any of the material I have about him."

Connor nodded grimly. "Everybody I interviewed refused to be named as a source and swore they'd deny everything if they were officially asked about Nollier or called upon to testify against him."

"Don't they realize their silence almost makes them accessories of that baby-selling barracuda?" Courtney exclaimed, frustrated.

"The adoptive parents are afraid of the consequences of an official investigation. They aren't exactly unaware that paying big bucks for a baby, directly to Nollier—all in cash, no records or receipts allowed—is legally questionable, at the very least."

"I've talked to some of the girls who gave up their babies and they wouldn't talk on the record, either," Courtney said quietly. "But they felt intimidated, even threatened, if they tried to change their minds about giving up their babies."

Connor frowned. "It looks like the only way to get some real evidence is to deal with Nollier directly." His eyes met Courtney's. "Maybe we don't have to compete, maybe we could work together on this, put together a plan and share information. Maybe *Insight, Inside Copy* and NPB could combine forces. *Insight* could do its usual two-page article, *Copy* its ten-minute quickie, and NPB could put together a serious documentary. Would you consider it, Courtney?"

It was a reasonable compromise. Wasn't it? "Well, maybe," she hedged, stalling.

"It would mean some role-playing, some under-cover investigating. Are you game, Courtney?"

Game-playing and undercover work. Had her over-active imagination gone wild or did that sound like a seductive, suggestive proposition? She swallowed, hard.

"Wilson Nollier is selling little babies to the highest bidder, Courtney," Connor continued, his green eyes intense. The story inflamed him. Even as he mocked himself for his single-mindedness on the subject, he still couldn't shrug it off.

"He's taking advantage of desperate couples who want children and can't have them naturally, people who have lost hope because of the adoption agencies' years-long waiting lists. And he's also victimizing desperate young women who find themselves pregnant and alone, maybe too poor or too young or emotionally unable to raise their babies. Those are the people that creeps like Nollier are preying upon."

Courtney stared at him in surprise. "You really care, don't you?" she said incredulously.

Connor's mouth curved faintly. "And that surprises you?" It certainly surprised the hell out of himself.

"Frankly, yes. You seem like the type of man who believes in feeling no pain, showing no fear or displaying no weakness. That type doesn't care about anyone or anything."

"You've pegged my character—or the lack of it—correctly, Gypsy," he admitted cheerfully. "Cool, cynical and shallow, avoiding emotional intimacy and involvement at all costs. That's me and I offer no apologies."

"But this baby-selling business has really gotten to you," she said, staring thoughtfully at him. Which called into question exactly how cool, cynical and shallow he exactly was.

Connor shrugged uncomfortably. "I just think it's unconscionable to sell human beings. And I hate seeing scum like Nollier parading around as a respectable member of the establishment while he's getting rich off defenseless people in desperate straits."

"So do I," she said softly.

"We can stop Nollier, Courtney." Connor's detached, sardonic expression disappeared and was replaced by one of genuine enthusiasm. "Working together we can infiltrate his adoption ring, gather the necessary evidence against him and then testify after charges are brought. We can bring him down, Gypsy, and get one helluva story in the process. Will you do it?"

Would she work with Connor McKay? Courtney found it unnerving that she found the prospect intriguing, especially when Connor was looking at her in *that* particular way, his eyes a breathtaking dark green, his handsome face alive with interest.

She immediately applied the mental brakes. "There are a few things I want to know before I commit myself to anything," she said, dampening her enthusiasm. It was essential to keep control of the situation, of herself!

"First of all, how will this story be presented by *Insight* and *Inside Copy?* If I use NPB time in and away from the office plus expense money for a documentary, I don't want *Inside Copy* or *Insight* coming up with some superficial, trashy angle on the whole story."

"I could always say that *Inside Copy* and *Insight* are never trashy or superficial," Connor began, his eyes gleaming.

Courtney folded her arms and regarded him archly. "Mmm-hmm."

"Or I could introduce you to the guy who'll write the story for *Insight* and you could talk to him about how it should be handled. He's their only correspondent based here in D.C. and he's one of the best writers in the news business."

"Which explains why he's working at *Insight,* that bastion of journalism, instead of at a lightweight organization like *The New York Times* or *The Washington Post.*"

"Touché." Connor smiled. "Your point, Courtney."

His smoky smile did queer things to her insides. Electricity flowed through her, sparking her nerves as his eyes traveled over her. The sensation was both unnerving and intriguing. Part of her wanted to look away sternly, the other part wanted to gaze deeply into those cool green eyes until—

Until what? demanded the other part of her, the non-whimsical, unromantic, reality-oriented side. Indulging in soulful stares with a smooth operator was a prescription for disaster. Her past experience with smooth operators was nonexistent, but one did not have to break a leg to know that it would hurt. The same metaphor also applied to hearts.

"We should meet with him as soon as possible," Connor said. "This afternoon."

"I can't just pick up and leave. I have things to do—"

"Put that fascinating special on the social habits of aardvarks on hold, Gypsy. We're about to begin the most important story that National Public Broadcasting has ever produced. And maybe the only relevant one," he added, a definite challenge in his tone.

She should ignore it and deal with him in the unemotional, businesslike manner with which she dealt with any other potential collaborator/colleague—she knew that. He was deliberately trying to get a rise out of her; Courtney knew that, too, but found it impossible not to respond in kind.

"I'm sick and tired of your malicious comments about NPB," she said fiercely. "If you don't stop making them, I'll refuse to even consider working with you."

"Too late, Gypsy. You've already considered—and agreed to do it." He grinned unrepentantly and handed her the uneaten portion of cheesesteak. "Now sit down and finish your lunch before we go. You're getting awfully cranky and no wonder—you haven't eaten since last night, remember? You have to keep up your strength."

"Spare me your phony concern," snapped Courtney. "Anyway, I've lost my appetite. You killed it," she couldn't resist adding. Her dark velvet eyes clashed with his.

A combination of instinct and experience told him that lunch was not the issue here. He read the message in her eyes. Though she might not even be aware of it, the challenge she was issuing was a feminine one. And his response was pure and primal male.

He cupped his big hands around her shoulders and carefully, but firmly, pushed her down into the chair. "There are a few ground rules that we should get straight since we're going to be working together," he said in a low, husky voice that rolled over her like a warm wave.

Courtney wriggled in her chair and tried to stand up, to assert her will, and most urgently, to put a safe and comfortable distance between them. His hands, still fastened on her shoulders, held her inexorably in the chair.

"Rule number one is that when I tell you to do something, you must do it." His voice was soft yet the edge of steel in it was unmistakable. "I'm putting myself in charge of our investigation because I'm familiar with the netherworld where dangerous rats like Wilson Nollier operate. You've been sheltered in your privileged ivory tower here, dealing with earnest and sincere do-gooders. You're no match for the opportunistic sleezeballs of the world."

"I'm no wide-eyed innocent who can be duped. *Or* threatened, especially by you!" she added succinctly.

She tried to rise again, this time with considerably more force. It was no use; her best efforts were hopeless against his masculine strength.

"Relax, Gypsy. I'm not threatening you." He began to knead her taut muscles with his fingers. She felt soft and delicate under his hands. His head lowered, and he accidentally brushed his chin against her sleek, dark hair. Or was it an accident? Her hair was soft and shiny and smelled wonderful. He inhaled deeply and almost closed his eyes. His head was starting to spin.

At first, Courtney sat quiescent under his hands while trying to assimilate the knowledge that she wasn't going anywhere unless he permitted it. It was an unsubtle display of the ease with which he could dominate her and a sour lesson for an independent woman accustomed to managing on her own.

But it was hard to preserve her angry reserve when his big, warm hands were on her. What had started as a tension-reducing massage had become slow, sensual, arousing caresses. She tried to sit straight and stiff in the chair, but maintaining an erect, tense posture was almost impossible with his fingers working their magic, when she could feel the heat emanating from his body and his warm breath fan her hair.

Courtney drew in a sharp, shaky breath and her heart seemed to jump in her chest. Had she imagined it or had his lips brushed the top of her head? She began to ache with the tension of holding back. She wanted to give in, to let her head fall back against the muscular wall of his chest. To close her eyes and relax...

Connor was waging a similar war with his own self-control. He'd already lost two major battles: the first, when he had looked into those great dark eyes of hers and succumbed to his sudden, overwhelming need to touch her, and the second by continuing to caress her, by keeping her locked under his hands.

He felt the slow, subtle beginning of her submission; her muscles were losing their tension, she was softening, leaning into his hands, her breathing quickening.

A sharp hot flame of desire flared through him. He could feel the heat, the pressure building within him, the pleasure knotting deep in his groin....

"Courtney!" The sharp, stern voice of Mimi Ditmar sounded outside the office, accompanied by an equally bone-jarring knock on the door.

Connor dropped his hands at the same moment that Courtney sprang from the chair. They moved swiftly to opposite ends of the office, as Mimi knocked again.

"Come in, Mimi," Courtney called in a voice that was embarrassingly, revealingly shaky. Her cheeks pinked, and she took great care not to glance in Connor's direction.

Mimi entered, carrying a stack of videotapes. "In view of Mr. McKay's interests in the American cinema, I thought he might like to see these tapes of our past shows dealing with the subject." She thrust them into Connor's hands. "Here you are, Mr. McKay. Take them with you and enjoy."

Connor looked completely baffled. Courtney smiled weakly. "Thank you, Mimi."

Mimi acknowledged her thanks with a brief nod, then briskly left the office.

"She thinks you're a filmmaker," Courtney explained before Connor could even ask. "A wild nonconformist Hollywood type. But she's obviously deemed you worthy of contributing to the network."

Connor arched his brows. "Any particular reason why she thinks that?"

Courtney responded with a silent shrug. She didn't care to inform him of her frantic rush to Mimi's desk which had led to the secretary's misapprehension. He would draw all the wrong conclusions.

She cast a quick, covert glance at him and found him watching her. Tension, thick and hot and almost tangible in its strength, stretched between them. Courtney knew he was remembering, as was she, those moments before Mimi's interruption. Once again heat flooded her. Thank heavens, he would never know how very close she had been to—to— "If you'll excuse me, I'd like to finish my lunch," she said quickly, interrupting her own sensual reverie. She would *not* permit herself to fall into the trap of spinning fantasies about a man like Connor McKay.

"I'll stay." He sat down in her chair again and picked up the American cinema transcript she had laid on her desk. "As soon as you're finished, we'll go see Kaufman. That's Kieran Kaufman, with *Insight* magazine," he added.

"I know that name. He's that local TV newscaster who keeps getting fired for one sleazy reason or another. *He's* the one who's going to write the adoption story?" She was not at all pleased by the news.

"Kaufman's trying to redeem himself. He's determined to put his days on the *Globe Star Probe* behind him and start afresh. Again."

"He worked for that scandal sheet? The *Globe Star Probe* is the slimiest, sleaziest tabloid of them all!"

"Give the guy a break, Gypsy. He's trying to climb up the ladder of respectability."

"You mean crawl, don't you? Or slither? That's the usual locomotion for reptiles."

Connor laughed. "You're a tough lady, Gypsy."

"And stop calling me Gypsy."

"I like it. It fits you."

"Yes, well, *snake* fits you, but I've managed to refrain from calling you that."

He laughed again, neither insulted nor wounded by the slur. When he settled himself more deeply in her chair and began to read the American cinema transcript, Courtney faced facts. Connor McKay was staying for as long as he chose—and when he left, she would go with him to meet her *Insight* collaborator.

How had it happened? she wondered. When had her compliance to his will become a fait accompli? It was too disconcerting to even think about. Courtney ate her lunch instead.

Three

Courtney stood beside Connor in the small cluttered office while *Insight*'s Kieran Kaufman subjected her to one of the most insultingly thorough once-overs she had ever been forced to endure. She stiffened with indignation and tried not to dwell on the strangely different response Connor's probing gaze had evoked within her earlier that day in her own office.

"Your newest babe?" Kaufman asked Connor.

"I wish." Connor laughed as he said it, but there was a hungry gleam in his eyes that sent a piercing frisson of heat straight to the core of her. "But Courtney has already set her cap for a high-class guy named Emery Harcourt."

Kaufman's ears perked up. "Harcourt. Of the Harcourt Foundation?"

"Surely *you* don't know the Harcourts?" For the life of her, Courtney could not envision the staid, genteel Harcourts having even a nodding acquaintance with a *Globe Star Probe* alumnus.

"I know everybody who's anybody," Kaufman boasted. "That is, I know *of* them. It's my business to know each and every potential source of scandal, whoever they may be."

"Not anymore, Kaufman. You're working for *Insight* now, not the *Globe Star Probe,* remember?" Connor reminded him dryly. "Courtney works for NPB and has been digging up facts about Wilson Nollier. We decided that instead of sabotaging each other's investigations, we should join forces and put Nollier permanently out of the baby-selling business."

"Ah, the Nollier story." Kieran Kaufman nodded knowingly. "This is the first time I've ever seen you take a personal interest in the facts you've uncovered, McKay. Don't you think you're getting a bit carried away? Just give me the stuff you've collected and I'll print it. There's no need to drag her and the pedantic NPB into it."

"You can't print the facts Connor has gathered because nobody has agreed to talk on the record," interjected Courtney.

"Like that's ever stopped me before," Kaufman chortled.

Courtney was scandalized. "I think *Insight* magazine made a big mistake when they hired you away from the *Globe Star Probe,*" she said sternly. "And I'll be making an even bigger one if I agree to collaborate with you in any way." She turned to Connor. "This just isn't going to work. I'm going to continue my research on my own." She strode quickly to the office door.

"Whoa! Don't go losing your temper again,

Gypsy.'' Laughing, Connor caught her around the waist, preventing her intended exit. "You're not going anywhere. Not yet."

Courtney gasped, outraged by his blatant show of masculine aggression. And unaccountably, embarrassingly, excited by it as well.

"We have to come up with some sort of strategy to put Wilson Nollier out of business permanently," Connor reminded her.

But it was hard to think of Wilson Nollier or anything else except how good it felt holding her like this. The low throb he had been feeling since he'd met her intensified in direct proportion to her nearness. She evoked strange but powerfully possessive feelings within him, elemental emotions he had never experienced before.

Courtney was suddenly breathless. The feel of his rugged, masculine frame was imprinted solidly against her back; she felt the muscular strength of his arms around her waist. Dangerous, heated sensations swirled and eddied through her.

Her head reflexively rolled back and came to rest momentarily on the satisfying, hard width of his chest. She felt surrounded by him, enveloped by his strong masculine warmth. She inhaled deeply, and his scent filled her nostrils, a drugging aroma of pure male virility.

A rush of sensual hunger, the likes of which she had never before experienced, jolted through her with such force that she gasped. Taut against her buttocks, she felt the unmistakable force of aroused maleness. An answering blaze kindled within her and she felt hot, so hot she feared that the flame might consume her.

Courtney let out a panicky sound, and her own hands covered Connor's, which were locked together over her stomach. She tried to pry his fingers loose.

"Let me go," she said in a husky voice that contained none of the authority she had intended and all of the shakiness she'd hoped to conceal.

But Connor obliged at once. He abruptly dropped his hands, releasing her, then sank into a nearby chair. She was definitely too hot to handle. In just those few minutes, his breathing had quickened, his heart rate had skyrocketed and the other physical effect she'd had on him was starkly visible.

Feeling uncharacteristically vulnerable, he snatched a copy of *Insight* magazine and placed it over his lap. "Sit down, Courtney," he ordered. "Kaufman, try to keep your *Probe* instincts under control and help us work out some kind of plan."

Courtney's first inclination was to run from the office. But then, that was what had caused Connor to grab her in the first place. Anyway, her knees felt peculiarly wobbly; she really needed to sit down. She dropped onto the hard, metal chair near the door.

"Damn, how did I get dragged into your personal crusade?" Kieran grumbled. "All I wanted was a sensational story. What's behind this vendetta against Nollier, anyway, McKay?"

"He wants to see justice served and to right a terrible wrong," Courtney spoke up. "That hardly falls within the realm of a personal vendetta, Mr. Kaufman." Why on earth was she leaping to Connor McKay's defense? she wondered, both annoyed and surprised that she had. The man was certainly capable of holding his own.

"Believe me, doll, I've been around long enough to

know that nothing is as simple as it seems," drawled Kaufman. "Serving justice and righting wrongs take second place to one's own agenda. Admit it, you have your own personal reasons for getting interested in the subject of adoption in the first place. You might as well 'fess up, because I'll find out anyway. Inquiring minds like mine want to know."

Courtney sighed impatiently. "It's no big secret why I happened to become interested in the subject of adoption. My older brother Mark and his wife Marianne have been trying to adopt a baby for the past five years and have been frustrated at every turn."

"So you hope to find a way to help them adopt a kid," Kaufman said with an I-told-you-so expression.

Courtney sighed. "Mark and Marianne have been on a number of adoption agencies' waiting lists, and they even applied to a surrogacy program three years ago. They paid a substantial fee and a young woman volunteer was chosen," she said, then paused, frowning. The story still had the power to upset her. "The woman was inseminated and became pregnant."

Connor leaned forward. "What happened?"

"Mark and Marianne were ecstatic about the pregnancy. And then the woman reneged." Courtney's face clouded. "Just a few weeks before the baby was due, she took off. She left a note saying that she couldn't bear to give up her baby and she's never been heard from again."

"Bummer," said Kieran. "Did your brother get his money back?"

"The director of the surrogacy program insisted that only half could be returned to them," said Courtney. "It was a big financial loss, but losing the money was nothing compared to losing the baby and knowing that Mark has a child out there he'll never know.''

"That's a damn shame, Courtney," murmured Connor.

"Yeah," Kieran agreed. "If they'd gotten the full amount back, they could've used it to buy a kid from Wilson Nollier's outfit.''

Connor and Courtney exchanged exasperated glances. "Kaufman, you've missed the point entirely," growled Connor. "And that happens to be, childless couples should not be exploited in their desire to have a family. Children are not commodities to be bought and sold.''

"Stop!" howled Kieran. "Save it for the righteous tearjerker of a program that'll undoubtedly air on NPB, courtesy of Miss Carey here. And now, let's hear your reasons for getting involved, McKay. But kindly skip the truth-justice-and-American-way lecture, because coming from you, I don't buy it.''

Connor stood up and began to pace the small office, reminding Courtney of a restless tiger in a too-small cage. "You're right, I do have a personal interest in the topic of Kids for Cash. The couple who raised me—my adoptive parents, if you will, although they never got around to formally filing adoption papers— were paid to take me. My biological father was a married man who'd had a fling that resulted in yours truly. He didn't want a scandal and gave the McKays a tidy sum to take me and keep things hushed up. Things were different thirty-four years ago. There was a surplus of adoptable infants and the McKays were in need of the cash.''

"How did you find out about all of this?" Courtney asked quietly. It was both an affecting and depressing revelation for anyone to learn about themselves, let alone cocky, confident Connor McKay. How strange, she thought; her brother and his wife would pay anything to obtain a child, but Connor McKay's adoptive parents had been paid to take him. Things certainly were different thirty-four years ago in the adoption market.

"My dad—the one who raised me, not the one who paid to get rid of me—told me when I turned thirteen," said Connor. "He figured I was old enough to know and had the right to learn the truth. My mother doesn't know I know the truth," he added. "I promised Dad I would go on pretending to believe the McKays are my natural parents. For some reason, Mom prefers the fiction to the truth."

"I don't know why he had to tell you the truth in the first place!" Courtney exclaimed indignantly. "It must have been a terrible shock, and he couldn't have picked a more sensitive age! The man sounds positively heartless. Was your mother cruel, too?"

Connor shook his head, laughing. "Don't get so rattled, Gypsy. My folks weren't cruel to me. Oh, there were some problems, sure. My dad was a compulsive gambler and regularly lost his paychecks at the track, but we never held that against him. He was a terrific father. He treated me no differently than he did his own two daughters, natural-born McKays who are two and three years younger than I am. Dad died of a heart attack six months ago," he added.

Dead or alive, Mr. McKay, Sr., didn't sound so terrific to Courtney. "What about your mother?" she asked curiously. "What was she like?"

"I was always closer to Dad than to my mother," Connor replied. "She wasn't as much fun, she always seemed preoccupied. Their marriage was on the rocks for as long as I can remember. Mom's a nurse and has always worked shifts at the local hospital, plus overtime. Anything to get out of the house, I think. There were times when we didn't see a whole lot of her.''

''No wonder she wasn't as much fun. She was unhappily married with three children and an irresponsible husband who gambled away his salary,'' Courtney felt compelled to point out. ''It's not surprising that the poor woman worked all the time. She had to! She was supporting the entire family.''

Connor shrugged and made no response. He'd already said enough, perhaps too much. He seldom talked about his family; he didn't care to reveal himself. He turned instead to Kaufman. ''Those are our respective motives for involving ourselves in the story, Kieran. I hope your inquiring mind is satisfied. Now it's time to formulate a plan.''

''I have an idea,'' Courtney said eagerly. ''I'll go to Wilson Nollier and tell him that I'm expecting a baby and want to give it up for adoption. Then we'll learn firsthand how he operates. I'll wear a wire to get everything he says on tape.''

''Give me a break!'' Kaufman snorted scornfully. ''Nollier is smart. He's not going to fall for a stupid, simplistic act like that. If you want to get him, you're going to have to play hardball, to put yourself on the line and be as deceptive and sophisticated as he is.''

''If you're going to suggest that I actually get pregnant to look more convincing, you can just forget it,'' Courtney said succinctly.

Connor turned to face her. ''I was thinking along the lines of you and I posing as a married couple, going to Nollier and telling him we want to adopt a baby. To nail Nollier for extortion, we have to be in the position where he can extort money from us—and that will be as potential adoptive parents.''

"No," Courtney said quickly. She didn't bother to question why playing the role of an unwed mother was less disconcerting, less threatening, than pretending to be married to Connor McKay.

"Faking a pregnancy is a lot more difficult than faking a marriage, Courtney," Connor cut in. "You'll need some sort of medical proof, and using bogus paperwork is a risk. Nollier has been successful in this adoption racket because he's careful. We can't risk losing credibility with faux documents. Adoptive parents don't need anything but cash. We'll pretend to be married and ask him to get us a child. We'll keep our own secret records for payments made to him and tape any incriminating conversations.''

Courtney considered it. As much as she hated to agree, his plan was better than hers, both easier and safer to enact. But the idea of pretending to be Connor's wife... She shifted restlessly and her eyes darted compulsively to him.

Their gazes met.

Courtney's breath caught in her throat. A tightness in her chest radiated lower, to her abdomen, and pierced her sharply, deeply. She tried to reason away the unreasonable, dangerous sexual excitement. There was no place in her life for a rogue like Connor McKay. The Connor McKays of the world caused women to read books on how to overcome heartbreak and to join support groups to cope with their misery.

"I'm only doing this for my brother and his wife and all the couples like them," she announced, as much for her own benefit as his. "If a creep like Nollier is put out of business, then maybe the birth mothers will give up their babies to legitimate sources and people without a fortune to spend will be able to adopt.''

Connor nodded, trying and failing to drag his eyes away from her. Another unwelcome flood of sensual hunger galvanized him, followed by a wave of confusion. He'd learned long ago not to pay too much attention to feelings and needs. It was easier and more convenient to keep them safely buried. But for the first time in years, he felt a break in his defensive wall. And that alarmed him.

''The two of you will certainly have fun playing married in that bucolic paradise, Shadyside Falls,'' Kaufman said, reasserting his presence with a leer.

''What are you talking about?'' demanded Courtney.

''We're not planning on going anywhere,'' added Connor.

''You don't know about Shadyside Falls?'' Kaufman heaved a sigh. ''Ah well, few can match me and my network of spies, I guess. The town of Shadyside Falls is the top-secret part of Nollier's operation.''

He regarded Connor and Courtney with undisguised superiority. ''Let me explain Wilson Nollier's usual procedure to you. Within a few weeks or months after the initial intake visit to his office in the city, Nollier insists that the prospective parents go to a small town named Shadyside Falls near the West Virginia-Maryland border.''

''Go away?'' echoed Courtney. ''The two of us? *Together?*''

Kaufman nodded. ''It's all part of the racket. Supposedly Nollier owns a big piece of this town. You'll stay in a place designated by him, and that's also where you'll get the baby. Meanwhile, you're under observation by *his* network of spies, so you'll have to be convincing. One of the reasons Nollier has yet to be nailed is because of this observation period. If there is a suspicion that the parents aren't exactly what they seem, they pay no money and get no baby. Or no evidence or story, either, of course. There can be no slipups or you're out, kids.''

''None of the couples I talked to mentioned this Shadyside Falls place,'' murmured Connor.

Privately he was shaken more than he ever cared to admit. It was one thing to pretend to be married to Courtney Carey in a lawyer's office. But to live with her while masquerading as husband and wife? The entire situation suddenly loomed as a particularly dangerous entanglement.

''The couples sign some kind of paper swearing to keep the Shadyside Falls experience confidential,'' said Kaufman.

''I'm not a lawyer, but even I know that such a paper isn't legal and binding,'' said Courtney. Her mind was reeling. *Live with Connor McKay as his wife? And convince any interested observers that they were happily married? Suppose their designated place to stay had one bedroom and one bed?*

''Sure, but it's proof of how scared of Nollier these couples are,'' said Kaufman. ''But they all recognize that the whole business is unethical and illegal and want to generate some heat, so they'll cooperate up to a certain point. If you really want to stop Nollier, you're going to have to go to Shadyside Falls to do it.''

"Of course we want to stop Nollier," said Court-ney.

Connor gazed into her beautiful dark eyes and felt a pang of guilt. Her reasons for wanting to stop Nollier were impeccable. He knew his were not. For beneath his contempt for Nollier's racket, he carried a personal grudge against the man as well. He was certain that Wilson Nollier had arranged his sale to the McKays.

Connor remembered the stunning pain he'd felt when he had first learned that he wasn't who he thought he was, that the McKays weren't his parents, that they had been paid to take him. And though he didn't reveal the identity of his birth mother, Dennis McKay had been eager to tell the thirteen-year-old about the wealthy, socially prominent executive who had fathered him and then given him away.

From that day on, Connor had read everything he could find about that man, his father, Richard Tre-maine. He knew where Tremaine lived and worked, knew that he had three half-brothers, Cole, two years older than himself, and Nathaniel and Tyler, both younger. He knew that Tremaine's wife Marnie—the one he'd cheated on—had been killed in a car accident at the age of twenty-nine. Tremaine had never remar-ried, but devoted himself to his company and to raising his three sons, all under eight at the time of their moth-er's death. Supposedly Tremaine had been shattered by his beautiful young wife's death and never consid-ered remarriage because he loved her still.

Connor scoffed at that fairy tale; his very existence disproved it. Richard Tremaine had cheated on the beautiful, tragic Marnie and his adulterous affair had produced an unwanted son.

It stood to reason that, thirty-four years ago, the

senior Tremaine would have called upon Wilson Nollier, his longtime lawyer-friend, to arrange the sale of his bastard son. Nollier and Tremaine had grown up together; they still golfed together and traveled in the same social circles. His old friend's fall would be a blow to Richard Tremaine, compliments of that same unacknowledged bastard.

"We're going to nail Nollier," Connor said fiercely, his green eyes glittering. "We'll do whatever it takes, won't we, Courtney?"

Courtney studied him. She was aware of a tension emanating from Connor, and it was different from the sexual tension that had stretched between them earlier. He looked dangerous, hard and cruel.

But crimes like baby-selling were cruel, and an adversary had to be tough to stand a chance of winning against a man like Wilson Nollier. If this expedition successfully ended Nollier's racket, it would be worth the sacrifice of enduring a few days of pretending to be Connor McKay's wife. After all, the key word was pretend. *And if there was only one bed, Connor could sleep in the bathtub or on the floor!*

"Yes, we'll do it," she affirmed, nodding her head.

"Fools rush in where angels fear to tread," Kaufman said laconically.

Courtney grimaced. She was uneasy enough; Kaufman's negative little digs didn't help. Once again, her eyes strayed to Connor, and once again, she caught him staring at her. Her pulse leaped.

"I have to leave," she announced suddenly. "I have an appointment in twenty minutes." A bit of a white lie; her appointment wasn't for another two hours. But every self-protective instinct she possessed clamored for her to get away. *Now.*

"I'll see you tonight," Connor called as she walked out the door. "Around eight. We have a lot of details to iron out."

"I have a date tonight. Give me a call at my office tomorrow," Courtney ordered and marched out.

"Sassy little wife you've got there, McKay," Kieran observed. "Needs to be shown who's boss."

Connor stared at the door, his eyes agleam. "I wonder if tonight would be too soon to start?"

No expense had been spared in feting the patrician Virginia horse breeder, Harmon Blake "Hop" Hopwood, on his sixtieth birthday. Courtney glanced around the enormous ballroom of the exclusive Twin Oaks Country Club, staring at the grove of real trees that had been embedded in concrete planters for the occasion and that gave the baroque ballroom the feel of an actual forest. Hop Hopwood was an avid outdoorsman, and the party decor reflected his tastes. The trees even had live wild birds in them, captured and housed in cages, a concession to the indoor aspect of the faux woodland setting.

A twenty-piece band provided music from the "big band" era, there was a sumptuous buffet and open bars and heavy socializing among the guests of all ages.

Courtney sat at a round table for eight, all the seats vacated but hers and Emery Harcourt's. Poor Emery hadn't wanted to come tonight, but his family had insisted, and he had obeyed, asking her to accompany him. His deepening depression concerned her. The appearance of his former fiancée with her new love had drained him of what little spirit he had. Courtney stayed by his side and tried to be consoling.

"Oh God, as if things weren't bad enough, here comes Jarrell," Emery said with a groan. "She's heading directly for our table."

Courtney stifled a groan of her own. He'd articulated her own thoughts exactly. They had already exchanged perfunctory hellos with Jarrell Harcourt earlier, and the woman had made no attempt to conceal her antipathy toward her brother's date. But here she was again, tall, slim and blond, her thick, straight hair styled in a classic bob. She was unsmiling, of course. As far as Courtney could tell, Jarrell Harcourt did not possess the ability to smile.

Jarrell joined them, taking a seat next to her brother, turned her back to Courtney and proceeded to converse with him. No one else came near the table, and Courtney, shut out of the Harcourts' conversation, sat in silence. Ten minutes crawled by, then fifteen. She sighed.

And then, just when she had decided that the interminable evening had reached its nadir, it took a definite turn for the worse.

For a moment, Courtney thought she was hallucinating. That couldn't be Connor McKay and Kieran Kaufman, in black tuxes and looking for all the world as if they belonged in this elite crowd, who were crossing the wide expanse of the ballroom. *Heading directly toward the table where she and the Harcourts sat.*

Courtney froze. She balled her hands into tight fists but barely felt her nails digging into her palms. Horror of horrors, it was McKay and Kaufman! And their elegant attire aside, the unholy grins on their faces were alarming testimony to the fact that they were up to no good.

"Uh, excuse me," Courtney mumbled and rose from the table. The dangerous duo were at least twelve feet away; if she moved swiftly she had enough time to intercept them before they reached the Harcourts.

"Hello, Gypsy." Connor's sea-green eyes slid lazily over her as she approached them.

Courtney was wearing an elegant peacock-blue silk dress that was cut in modest, classic lines and was not the least bit gypsylike. Her dark eyes smoldered. "What are you doing here?"

"I guess you wouldn't believe that we were invited? That we're old golfing buddies of Hop's?" drawled Connor.

"I most certainly would not. You crashed this party!"

"Bingo!" Kaufman exclaimed.

Courtney sent him a scathing glance, then turned to Connor again. "Why did you crash the party?" A dreadful thought struck her. "Surely not to—to see me?"

"I told you we needed to talk tonight," Connor replied, shrugging. "Since you insisted on being here, it was only logical that we hold our meeting here. Although I can't say much for the surroundings." He glanced around him, his expression disapproving. "Trapping those poor birds and shutting them up in cages so these society geeks can gawk at them..." He shook his head. "I know a few diehard animal rights activists. Maybe I should give them a call and alert them to this abuse."

"Get them and their pickets over here right away," Kieran said gleefully. "I'll call a local news team who is sympathetic to the cause. It might make the news at eleven."

"No!" cried Courtney. But what was even more horrifying than the thought of a fanatical group of picketers and camera crew crashing the party was the fact that Connor McKay had just spoken the very thoughts she'd been harboring all evening about those poor captive birds. She did not want to be so psychically attuned to him!

"How did you know I was here?" she demanded nervously.

The two men looked at each other, then back at her. "It's part of my job to track people down, Gypsy," Connor explained with a patient air that she found extremely irritating. "I've traced reclusive celebrities who cover their trails with professional expertise, and I've traced politicians holed up with women who were most definitely not their wives, to mention just a few cases. Locating you was a kindergarten exercise."

"Hey, who's the blond babe sitting at your table?" Kieran asked, surveying the crowd with his weasel-sharp eyes.

Courtney actually smiled. "That's Jarrell Harcourt. And I'm willing to bet that's the first time in her life she's ever been referred to as a 'babe.'"

Kaufman stared, assessing the woman. "Hmm. Looks tense and humorless—but sexy in a snobbish, aristocratic kind of way. Desperately needs to get laid, I wager. Well, this is her lucky night. I'm going to blitzkrieg her. She'll never know what hit her until she wakes up tomorrow morning in my bed." He headed purposefully toward the table.

"*Blitzkrieg?*" Courtney echoed, staring after him.

Connor wrapped his fingers around her wrist, effectively manacling her. "It's no use trying to stop him,

Gypsy. Kaufman is like a guided missile—once fired, nothing can deflect him from his trajectory.''

"Oh, I wasn't going to try to stop him,'' Courtney said dryly. "If there were ever two people in the world who deserved to meet, it's those two.''

"Wicked, Gypsy.'' Connor grinned. His eyes narrowed as he followed Kaufman's progress to the Harcourt's table. "I take it that's your boyfriend, the inestimable Emery, sitting there?''

"That's Emery,'' Courtney agreed, not bothering to correct his misassumption. It seemed wiser—and safer—not to.

"He's kind of pale. Is he anemic?''

"Not that I know of.''

"He's not exactly the life of the party, is he? In fact, he looks so morose he could hire himself out as a professional mourner at funerals.''

It was an unfortunately astute observation, but loyalty to poor unhappy Emery kept Courtney from agreeing. "I'm not going to stand here and listen to you rip Emery to shreds. He doesn't deserve it. And I'd like my hand back, if you don't mind.'' She tried to pull her wrist out of his grip, to no avail. It was like trying to shake off a locked handcuff.

"I was simply stating a few facts about Master Emery, not attacking his undoubtedly sterling character,'' Connor said coolly. He released her wrist. The way she leapt to Harcourt's defense was annoying. The fact that he found it annoying was even worse. His lips thinned into a straight line. "But we've wasted enough time—we have to discuss our visit to Nollier's office tomorrow.''

"Tomorrow?'' Courtney repeated. Her dark eyes widened. "I didn't realize we'd start so soon.''

"The sooner the better," he said briskly. "I called Nollier's office this afternoon and set up an appointment for tomorrow at one. His secretary put me through to him and I spoke to him personally. He said to prepare to leave for Shadyside Falls after our meeting tomorrow afternoon."

"Tomorrow?" Courtney echoed incredulously. "But Kaufman said couples went to Shadyside Falls weeks or months after their initial visit."

Connor shrugged. "Nollier said our timing is incredibly lucky." He smiled a shark's smile. "And it is, but not for him."

Courtney gulped. "I—I'll have to make arrangements with my boss to spend time away from the office."

"Will that be a problem?"

"No." She shook her head. "But do you really think that we should rush into this? I mean, we only decided to do it today and—"

"In the immortal words of Kieran Kaufman, 'Fools rush in, etcetera.'" Connor's voice lowered. "Getting cold feet, Gypsy? Maybe you can't trust yourself to play the role of my wife without wanting to—"

"Don't say it!" Courtney said hotly. "Don't even think it!"

Connor laughed, his earlier irritation dissolving as he gazed into the fiery dark depths of her eyes. She amused him, excited him as no woman ever had. And tonight, his trusty bachelor alarm failed to sound. He felt cocky and dangerous, he felt like taking a few risks.

"Let's go out on the terrace and talk all about tomorrow, Courtney." He took a step toward her.

Courtney took a step back. She had seen the long

terrace that lined the outside of the ballroom when she'd arrived with Emery. It was dark, lit only by the moon and stars. And it was secluded. A couple could be completely alone and unobserved out there....

She took another step backward. Her eyes met Connor's and a slow smile crossed his face.

"Keep walking, Gypsy." He provided the necessary incentive by walking toward her. "Just keep on going. The terrace is only a couple hundred steps away."

Four

She could always stop moving, Courtney thought, even as she kept backing up. The problem with that plan, however, was that Connor didn't give any indication that he would stop coming toward her. If she were to stop, it appeared in all likelihood that he would crash right into her.

"I'm not going to let you bully me," she announced, while walking backward at a rather hasty clip.

"Good for you. I like a woman who stands up for herself."

He was bullying her *and* mocking her. Once again Courtney felt her temper, usually so even, so mild and easy to control, begin to rise to flaring heights. "I'm going to stand still, right here, right now," she announced sharply.

She stopped moving and stood stock-still. To her

delight, Connor stopped too. Proud of herself, Courtney shot him a triumphant look.

Connor shrugged. "We can talk here as well as anywhere, Gypsy."

He appeared completely nonchalant, and Courtney might have been lulled into complacency had she not caught a swift glimpse of the wild, hot and hungry gleam in his eyes.

Her sense of victory faded abruptly. They were standing face-to-face, only a few inches apart. She glanced nervously around at their surroundings; somehow they'd ended up in the thick grove of trees lining the ballroom. They were concealed from the others, though the loud party sounds disrupted the illusion of the primeval forest.

"But first things first," Connor continued softly, lacing his long fingers through her thick dark hair. He tilted her face up to him at the same moment that his head descended toward her. "This has been simmering between us all day. Let's get it out of our systems now."

"Out of our systems?" she echoed. Her mind wasn't working as quickly as it should. Neither was the rest of her. She should be slapping him away and fleeing this too-private indoor wooded glen. Courtney knew all that, but somehow she remained where she was, which was far too close to Connor McKay.

While she was wondering if she should blame her sudden mental and physical lethargy on the glass of champagne she had consumed earlier this evening, Connor lightly touched his mouth to hers.

The feel of his lips, warm and firm against hers, galvanized her into action. She drew back her head and placed both her hands on his chest, in an attempt to keep him literally at arm's length. "Stop it, Connor. I know what you're doing."

"Mmm, I thought you might." He wrapped his arms around her, and her elbows flexed from the pressure he exerted to draw her closer to him. Suddenly she was not even a hand's length away from him.

Courtney drew a sharp breath. She was intensely aware of his size and strength, of the heat of his hard body. For one breathless, insane moment, she felt the urge to lean into all that masculine heat and strength, to relax against him and let him support her....

Quickly she pulled her head back farther, turning her face away from him. "Let me go, Connor."

Denied her lips, he sought the slender, sensitive curve of her neck and began to nibble. "But I don't want to let you go, Courtney."

It annoyed her that he was not taking her refusal or her demand seriously. And she should be far more than annoyed with him, Courtney acknowledged grimly. She should be furiously fighting this type of caveman machismo; at the very least, she ought to be a little afraid of his physical power. But for reasons she didn't care to delve into, she was neither infuriated nor afraid.

Defensively Courtney scowled up at him. "You're trying to *blitzkrieg* me."

He smiled, a slow, lazy, sexy smile that made her heart turn over. "Bombs away," he said huskily, and his mouth closed over hers.

In the nick of time Courtney pressed her lips tightly together, effectively denying him access to her mouth's interior. She heard the muffled sound of frustration he made against her closed mouth and couldn't help smiling.

Connor lifted his mouth a quarter inch above hers.
"Ah, Gypsy, you don't play fair," he murmured
against her lips, feathering the curve of her mouth with
his lips, with the tip of his tongue. "This is supposed
to be a blitzkrieg, not a siege." His hands slid intimately over her body.

Molded against him, Courtney felt the burgeoning
pressure of his thighs against her. Her breasts were
cushioning the muscular wall of his chest. Maybe she
was going to have to cling to him for support after all,
for her legs felt almost too weak for her to remain
standing.

"Open your mouth for me, Courtney." Connor's
voice was deep and thick.

His words, bold, intimate and demanding, sent her
pulse rate out of control. Sweet, hot rivers of sensation
flowed through her, deep and thrilling. If she were to
let go, reason and willpower would be swept away in
those seductive currents. The temptation to cede all
control, to close her eyes and open her mouth and let
him take her over, was almost irresistible.

Alarmingly so. She was just a hairbreadth away
from allowing herself to be carried away by a tide of
passion, when the shock of surrender set her meta-
phorically, but firmly, back on high ground.

As an army brat who'd moved from place to place
and friend to friend, she had become independent and
self-reliant at an early age. Those character traits, cou-
pled by her strong will and fierce penchant for self-
control, did not make it easy for her to acknowledge
that she was dangerously close to submission, however
sublime it promised to be.

Her dark eyes, heavy-lidded and half-closed,
snapped wide open. She stared up at Connor, who was

watching her with intense sea-green eyes. He wanted her. There could be no denying the blatant physical evidence of his desire. But she saw more than passion glittering in those beautiful eyes of his—she saw challenge as well. And if she were to melt into him and kiss him the way he wanted—*the way she wanted him to!*—that challenge would be replaced by pure male triumph.

She recognized in that instant that Connor McKay had a will as strong as her own, that his self-control rivaled, maybe even surpassed, hers. For *he* was not the one on the verge of giving into the heady temptation of passion. He was in full control of himself, of her, and of this premeditated little tryst in the middle of a fake forest.

Courtney stiffened. "Give it up, Connor," she said tautly. "It's not going to work."

Their faces were so close, their lips an inch apart. When Connor smiled, she could almost feel the warm, full curve of his mouth on hers. She wanted to feel it. Courtney was aghast at just how badly she wanted it.

"Give up now? Why should I, Gypsy? I have you right where I want you—and right where you want to be."

She was furious, partly with him but mostly with her newly discovered sensual self, who was proving to be an embarrassingly unreliable ally. And she would never admit that his arrogant taunt happened to be the truth.

"Your ego must be the size of Jupiter if you believe that I want to be manhandled in the midst of a bunch of potted trees." She flung the words at him, seething with temper. "Furthermore, I happen to be here with another man, remember?"

It was about time *she* remembered that fact, Courtney scolded herself. She'd been so absorbed with Connor, she'd scarcely given poor morose Emery a thought.

Connor frowned. The mere mention of her date sent flames of jealousy roaring through him. *And he was not a jealous man!*

"You want me," he growled. "You're just too stubborn to admit it."

"I'll admit that you threw me off balance with your seduction skills. They were quite effective—for a minute or two. Then I recovered."

"A minute or two?" Connor repeated indignantly. He glared into her upturned, defiant small face. Unfortunately it seemed that she actually had had a complete recovery from the soft, submissive woman she'd been only a few moments ago. Right before his eyes, she had turned into a sharp-tongued, argumentative termagant. Connor was not pleased with the transformation.

"Are you going to let me go?" She had an older brother and two older stepbrothers; she knew something about threats and intimidation, both making them and not bowing to either.

"No," Connor replied succinctly.

She knew exactly what to say next. "Then I'll have to *make* you let go of me."

"And how will you do that?" Connor taunted, deliberately tightening his hold on her. A tactical mistake on his part, he silently conceded, for the feel of her softness against him was making his already-fevered blood run even hotter.

"Are you a graduate of one of those feminist self-defense courses?" he murmured mockingly. "What's your move, Gypsy? Going to deliver a neck-cracking karate chop that'll leave me rolling on the ground, begging for mercy?"

"I'm sorry I didn't take one of those courses," Courtney snapped. He obviously wasn't going to let her go and now she had to back up her tough words with action. But how? "If I had, I wouldn't show you any mercy," she continued with vicarious ruthlessness. "I'd make sure you were—"

"So, no karate chop," he cut in. "Perhaps you'll go with a less-sophisticated maneuver like that old classic, the swift knee to the groin?" Before she could attempt to do it, he closed his thighs around hers, immobilizing her—and sending shock waves of erotic sensation through them both.

For a moment they stood still, helpless against the tide of desire and need pulsing through them. Their eyes met and held and neither spoke a word.

He cupped her bottom with his palms and locked her tighter into his body. "You don't really want to put me out of commission, do you, Gyps?" he whispered against her ear. His tongue traced its delicate shape.

Courtney whimpered. That dangerous, languorous weakness had returned, seeping thickly into her limbs. There was a sharp sweet ache in the pit of her stomach. Being so very close to him, she could feel his body trembling, hear him drawing deep, uneven breaths. Though she didn't know how or why, she sensed a vulnerability in him that matched her own.

He was not just playing games, every feminine instinct she possessed informed her of that. He wanted her very, very badly. The knowledge was electrifying, so was the feel of her breasts nestled against his chest and the rhythmic throbbing of his unyielding virility. Courtney's head spun. What if she were to let go and kiss him, just once....

Her lips parted and his mouth lowered to hers.

"Look out!" The sharp warning voice seemed to come from another dimension.

Startled beyond measure, Courtney and Connor reflexively sprang apart. A low-flying bird, chirping madly, flew over their heads. Then another bird flew by, leaving a thick dropping that landed perilously close to where the two of them had been standing entwined.

"Damn birds." Kieran Kaufman joined them, glaring up at the twittering, fluttering avian pair that had perched on an overhead branch. "I never would've let them out if I thought they were going to go ballistic."

Courtney was shaking; she couldn't seem to stop. Desire bubbled through her, hot and swift and unquenched. She glanced quickly at Connor. He was staring purposefully into the branches of the trees.

"You let the birds out of the cages?" Connor asked Kaufman. Frustrating as the interruption had been, he was strangely grateful for it. He felt confused and off balance, a totally new experience for him and, he decided, a terrible one.

Never had he been so stirred, so aroused, by simply holding a woman, by the mere prospect of a kiss. When Courtney had gazed up at him, acquiescence in her dark velvet eyes, her lips parted and moist, he'd felt as if the top of his head had been blown off. Imagine what would have happened to him if he had actually kissed her.

It was definitely time to back up and regroup his defenses. The little spitfire was a living, breathing danger zone. No woman had ever affected him so profoundly, and he was damned if he would let this one get to him. *Especially not this one!* She was everything he didn't like, he reminded himself, an uptight, quarrelsome, stuck-up intellectual who considered a twit like Emery Harcourt to be the man of her dreams!

"I opened every bird cage I saw," Kieran confessed blithely. "I don't think anybody's noticed yet. When I saw that bird heading directly at you, I thought I better warn you. Sorry if I interrupted anything."

Courtney finally found her voice. "You didn't," she said quickly.

"No," Connor agreed, just as swiftly. "You didn't interrupt a thing."

A shout sounded from beyond the trees, followed by a shriek. "Uh-oh, I think the party guests just realized that their decorations are on the loose," said Kieran. "Definitely time to split. Hey, Connor, old pal, I know I drove us here, but can you find a ride home? I'm leaving with my hot new babe." He smiled wolfishly. "We're heading to my place now." He turned and dashed through the trees.

"I—I'd better get back to Emery," Courtney murmured. She kept her eyes carefully averted from Connor, not daring to look at him. She simply couldn't, not after what had just happened between them. A hot blush suffused her whole body. After the way she'd protested and threatened, to have finally succumbed to him...

For it was no use kidding herself. She'd been lost at the end, savoring the hard feel of his body against her, hungering to feel his mouth on hers. A mortified moan escaped from her throat as she rushed blindly back to the table.

There, to her utter incredulity, she saw Kieran Kaufman slipping his arm around the elegant, austere and forbidding Jarrell Harcourt—who was suddenly looking neither austere nor forbidding. Courtney blinked. Jarrell's cheeks were flushed, her eyes bright; she looked nervous and excited and much younger than her twenty-four years.

Courtney met Emery's curious gaze, then they both watched Kaufman's hand curve audaciously around the young woman's buttocks as he led her away. Jarrell's girlish giggle seemed to hang in the air. Jarrell Harcourt, the woman who never smiled, had actually *giggled!* Courtney decided her mind was truly blown.

"Who is that man?" Emery asked. "It was rather phenomenal watching him turn on the charm. Jarrell melted like a crayon in the sun. I've never seen her react like that to anyone."

"Charm?" Courtney echoed in disbelief. He had to be joking! She debated sharing Kaufman's identity with Emery and decided against it. Hadn't the poor man suffered enough tonight without having to hear that his sister had taken off with one of the sleaziest reporters in the business?

"Emery Harcourt!" The sound of Connor's voice, in a hearty hail-fellow-well-met tone, abruptly erased the astonishing alliance of Kaufman and Jarrell from Courtney's thoughts. She whirled around to see Connor extending his hand to Emery to shake.

"I'll give you ten-to-one odds you don't remember me," said Connor as he pumped the hand Emery offered to him.

Emery smiled vaguely. "I'm not a gambling man, but I'm terribly sorry, I can't quite place you."

Courtney tensed. What was Connor McKay up to

now? She glared at him, but he ignored her, smiling a broad smile that she *knew* was phony.

"We prepped together, Emery," Connor said easily. "But I was one of those quiet, nondescript guys who nobody ever remembers."

Courtney smoldered. After that pseudo-humble remark, what else could sweet, sensitive Emery say but, "Of course I remember you. But you know me, I've always been terrible with names."

"Connor McKay," Connor supplied smoothly.

Emery smiled and nodded. "McKay, of course! How have you been?"

"McKay hasn't been well at all," Courtney inserted frostily. "In fact, he just got out of prison."

She placed a protective hand on Emery's arm. He was so naive and trusting. Anyone who thought Kieran Kaufman was charming needed her protection, especially from a manipulative snake like Connor McKay. "Let's call it a night, Emery," she suggested sweetly. "I have an early appointment tomorrow."

Emery cleared his throat. "Courtney, if you don't mind, I'd like to get reacquainted with my old friend here." Emery, forever the well-brought up gentleman, offered Connor a chair. "Prison, hmm? Tough break, McKay."

"Junk bonds," Connor said, sitting down at the table, but not before shooting Courtney a mocking, victorious grin. "I didn't know what my tax attorney was up to, but I took the fall. It's been tough, all right. Former friends don't want to give you the time of day after you've served time."

"There's one thing you can count on from a Harcourt and that's loyalty," Emery said fervently, glancing at Courtney with silent reproof.

"Have a seat, Courtney," Connor invited. "Unless, of course, you don't want to sit at a table with an ex-con. I'll understand completely if you don't."

"Don't ever think such a thing," Emery exclaimed. "I'm quite sure Courtney joins me in welcoming you back. She is quite a fair-minded egalitarian."

"Harcourt's a nice guy," Connor admitted grudgingly fifteen minutes later as he and Courtney made their way through the ballroom, which was still in the throes of pandemonium, courtesy of Kieran Kaufman's bird-releasing spree.

The feathered escapees flew helter-skelter through the room, and many of the guests already had departed in panic. Courtney wished that she had been among them. Instead, she had remained at the table while Connor and Emery conversed. She was still wondering why she'd stayed, silently listening to Connor use his considerable, subtle investigating skills to ferret out the details of Emery's life.

What was it about Connor McKay that compelled her to go along with him, when common sense urged her to beat a hasty retreat? she wondered nervously. Instead of ejecting him from her office today, she'd allowed him to stay. Instead of telling him to get lost, she'd agreed to collaborate with him. And now tonight, instead of informing Emery that he had *not* prepped with Connor McKay—who also wasn't a yuppie felon—she had sat quiescently and listened in fascination as he drew information about the Harcourts with skills that would have done any prosecuting attorney proud. He had even weaseled a ride home!

Still, she'd said nothing, allowing the unsuspecting Emery to go for his car, leaving her alone with Connor

McKay. *Three strikes and you're out,* she reminded herself, involuntarily glancing at him, taking in his sandy brown hair, still tousled from their little match under the trees, his deep green eyes, and his well-shaped, sensually compelling mouth. She swallowed, hard.

"I can see why you two have never made it to bed, though," Connor continued thoughtfully, his voice breaking into her troublesome reverie. "I've never heard a guy in love refer to his woman as a fair-minded egalitarian. Not very romantic, Gypsy."

"Maybe not by *your* standards," Courtney retorted. Or by anyone else's, either, she silently conceded. But then Emery wasn't in love with her, she wasn't his woman, and neither of them had ever pretended otherwise. Until now, with this stupid ruse she was playing at Connor's expense. Poor Emery would be horrified at the deception. She considered telling Connor the truth about the two of them, then decided against it. The man was too smugly confident, too arrogant. He deserved to be deceived!

A peculiar flashback of Connor telling her and Kaufman about being sold as an infant suddenly appeared before her mind's eye. He hadn't looked arrogant or smug then. The bleakness in his eyes, in his tone, had touched a chord deep within her. She determinedly shook off the feeling, which had returned in full. She felt sorry for the hurt young boy he had been then, she assured herself. For the current Connor, she felt only hostility.

They reached the spacious lobby of the club. It's hushed, solemn atmosphere was a distinct change from the noisy melee in the ballroom.

"But I still don't understand it." Connor shook his

head, still pondering her alleged relationship with Emery Harcourt. "You're so damn sexy, and Harcourt seems like a normal functioning male, yet—"

"In case it hasn't occurred to you, my relationship with Emery is absolutely none of your business," Courtney interrupted crossly. "And since I do not appreciate your speculations on my—"

"Sex life?" It was Connor's turn to interrupt and he did so, with unabashed glee. "Baby, you don't seem to have one."

She knew he was teasing her, but if he only knew how on target he really was! Courtney remembered all the virginity jokes she had endured in college when she had been foolish enough to confess she'd never had a lover. Now, as the only twenty-five-year-old virgin in the United States—perhaps in all of Western civilization—she kept her status a closely guarded secret.

"I'm sure no one has the peripatetic, athletic and feckless sex life that you undoubtedly indulge in, but what discriminating person wants to?" she snapped.

From his expertise in the faux grove, she deduced that all too many women had experienced his compelling sexual charisma. Her lips tightened.

"You really zinged me with that one, Gyps." Connor laughed appreciatively. "Nice hit."

His good-natured laughter increased her ire. She was also offended that *he* was not offended by her description of his life-style. He made it quite clear that he didn't care what she thought of him.

"Oh, shut up and leave me alone," she said coldly, storming across the lobby, away from him.

Connor immediately joined her. He couldn't keep

away from her, he enjoyed needling her too much; he enjoyed the way she held her own with him.

"I know you're not a member of my fan club, Courtney." His smile was more of a smirk, further escalating her blood pressure. "I'm not exactly a fan of yours, either. But since we're going to be working together, let's try to keep our mutual aversion under control, shall we?"

She was working on a suitable rejoinder when his expression, his posture, his entire demeanor suddenly changed. Courtney stared at him curiously. As if by the stroke of some magic wand, the laid-back, grinning tease had vanished, replaced with a tense, rigid and remote stranger.

"See that man coming through the archway?" he asked.

His voice contained some indescribable note, something inexplicable that put her instantly on alert. She followed his line of vision and spied a tall, distinguished-looking man, probably in his early sixties, with well-defined features and a full head of silver hair. He was impeccably dressed in a charcoal gray suit that even to her untutored eye looked custommade.

"That's Richard Tremaine," Connor said in that same strange tone. "Principal stockholder and CEO of Tremaine Incorporated."

Courtney nodded. Who in the Washington area didn't know of Tremaine Incorporated, a multimillion-dollar family company that owned a phenomenally successful chain of discount drugstores plus a popular chain of bookstores?

"Tremaine Incorporated gave a big grant to NPB this year," she told Connor. "We used it to produce a wonderful documentary on the foliage in a Central American tropical rain forest." She waited expectantly for his sarcastic remark about the program. Amazingly enough, he didn't make one. Could it be that he found the topic interesting?

"I'm going to go over there and thank Mr. Tremaine personally," Courtney decided impulsively.

"You mean you're going to suck up to him, hit him up for some more cash," Connor jeered. "At least be honest with yourself and own up to your true motives, Gypsy." His face was hard, his eyes dark and cold.

Courtney flinched. His accusation hurt more than angered her. "I don't have to stand here and be insulted by you," she said tightly.

Obviously Connor had some grudge against hardworking, achieving members of the establishment, she decided, thus his hostility toward Richard Tremaine. She frowned. Given Connor's idiotic job—straddling private investigating and reporting but not following through in either—she shouldn't be surprised by his resentment of conventional success.

Well, *she* was a staunch admirer of it. Holding her head high, Courtney crossed the lobby and introduced herself to Richard Tremaine.

He was kind and courtly and graciously responded to her introduction and her thanks. They chatted pleasantly about NPB and its goals, and Courtney assured herself that she was *not* sucking up to Mr. Tremaine, as Connor had so crudely accused. It was simply good manners to show appreciation for a gift.

A few minutes later they were joined by a taller, younger and even more handsome version of Richard Tremaine. Courtney was introduced to his eldest son Cole, and Cole's striking redhaired wife, Chelsea. The younger Tremaine sons, Nathaniel and Tyler, two more dark-haired Adonises, joined them shortly afterward with their dates, and once again introductions were made all around.

"I wonder who really did open those bird cages?" Tyler flashed a smile at his brothers. A smile that made Courtney stare hard at him. There was *something* about his smile...

"So far I've heard at least fifteen different people claim credit for doing it, but I don't believe any of them," said Cole, affectionately lacing his fingers with his wife's. "Not one has the nerve to jaywalk, let alone turn Hop's birthday party into a scene from Hitchcock's *The Birds.*"

The lobby was rapidly filling with refugees from the party. The wild birds had won control of the ballroom, driving everybody else out. As the Tremaines continued jokingly to speculate on the identity of the bird liberator, Courtney decided it was definitely time to fade into the crowd. With any luck, they never would find out who the real culprit was or her unfortunate connection to him. She excused herself and slipped away.

She looked for Connor, but he was nowhere to be seen. She was irritated to find him standing outside the club, talking to a glamorous brunette who was making a meal of him with her big, overly made-up eyes.

"Is Emery here with the car yet?" she asked, coming to stand between Connor and Cleopatra Eyes. Both of them welcomed her with the enthusiasm of vacationers faced with a bag of medical waste washed up on shore, which inspired Courtney to make an even greater pest of herself.

"I just had the nicest talk with the Tremaines.

They're four of the handsomest men I've ever met, but the middle son, Tyler, is to-die-for,'' she prattled on. She normally eschewed such slang as "to-die-for," but she decided it worked quite nicely tonight.

Connor's attention immediately shifted from the brunette to Courtney. "Tyler Tremaine is way out of your league, honey," he said tautly.

Courtney flashed what she hoped was an enigmatic smile. "Oh, I don't think so."

She watched with satisfaction as he turned his back on his new chum to focus completely on her. "Did he ask you out?" he demanded.

"Here's Emery," Courtney sang out and sailed down the wide stone steps.

Connor dogged her heels. "Did he?" he demanded. His heart was pumping at an alarming speed. Tyler Tremaine—his own half-brother—and *Courtney?* He felt a shocking wave of fury wash over him, followed by another of pure despair. He caught her arm, just as she was about to open the car door.

Courtney was grinning. "Did you see the way Cleopatra up there was glowering?" She didn't bother to question why diverting his attention from the other woman should make her feel so gloriously happy. "If looks could kill, I'd be on a life-support system."

"Stay away from Tyler Tremaine. And from all of the Tremaines," Connor said hoarsely. His fingers tightened on her arm.

"Let me go!"

"I'm serious, Courtney. You will not have anything to do with Tyler Tremaine."

He had watched her talking and smiling with his father, with his brothers, and the sight had shaken him profoundly. She'd looked as if she fit in with them, as if she belonged. He could imagine her discussing art with his father, who, he knew, had a sizable collection of modern paintings. He could see her chatting cozily about babies with Chelsea Tremaine, who a year ago had given birth to little Daniel Richard—the nephew he would never know, just as he'd never known his father or his brothers.

And as he had stood there, watching her with the Tremaines, imagining all sorts of scenes that would never come true, the intensity of the feelings coursing through him had made him wonder if he were on the verge of totally losing it. He'd made it a habit not to feel, a career of keeping longing and emotion at bay. Now his internal walls seemed to be cracking and he'd rushed away in alarm.

But there was no escape. Nothing he had ever experienced compared to the riot going on inside him at the thought of Tyler with Courtney. His brothers had had everything their entire lives, including their natural father, who'd claimed them and given them his name. Tyler Tremaine was not going to have his Gypsy!

His? Connor froze. This unprecedented attack of possessive jealousy unnerved him more than anything else. He released her arm from his grasp and backed away from her, as if she were emitting radioactive rays.

Courtney watched him curiously, wondering at the range of emotions flickering in his eyes. He tried so hard to be cool and unreadable; now he was anything but. His intensity disturbed her as much as it did him, and she sought to lighten the mood. And to reassure him?

"You certainly have an exaggerated estimation of

my appeal," she said wryly. "Tyler Tremaine could date movie stars if he wanted, he'd hardly pick me. Oh, and let's not forget my relationship with Emery— who is waiting so patiently while we're standing here, tying up traffic." She quickly hopped into the front seat of the car.

A moment later, Connor climbed into the back. He didn't say one word the entire way home, although Emery tried to include him in the conversation by offering some hilarious prep school reminiscences he assumed they shared.

Five

Her stepsister Michelle was sitting on the sofa watching television when Courtney let herself into her apartment. She suppressed a groan. It wasn't that she was not enjoying Michelle's visit; it was just that she would have preferred to slip into bed without a postmortem of tonight's events. How could Courtney offer up a comprehensible summation of the evening when she couldn't begin to make sense of it or her own surging emotions?

"Hi!" Michelle smiled warmly at her. "How was the party?"

Her stepsister was always so genuinely glad to see her. Courtney felt a twinge of guilt for even momentarily wishing Michelle back in her own Harrisburg apartment. She flopped down onto the sofa and managed a smile of her own. "It was—uh—" *An adjec-*

tive, Courtney. Find an adjective. She cleared her throat. "Interesting."

Michelle chuckled. "That covers a lot of territory, from the sublime to the pits of horror. I know. I've spent some *interesting* evenings myself. Emery seems nice," she offered. They'd met when he had come to pick up Courtney this evening. "Have you been dating him long?"

"I'm not dating him at all, Michelle. That is, not in the way that you mean. We're strictly friends and will never be anything more." An idea suddenly occurred to her. "Maybe you'd like to go out with Emery while you're here? As you said, he's very nice, a perfect gentleman. He's quite intelligent, a terrific conversationalist and definitely available. I don't know why I didn't think of this before. You'd be ideal together."

"Courtney, I wouldn't be ideal with anyone," Michelle protested with a slight laugh. "Not now." She stood up and walked out of the room.

Courtney followed her. Michelle had gone into the kitchen and was petting her Siamese cat, Burton, who was lounging on a place mat on the kitchen table. Michelle always traveled with whatever pet cat she happened to own at the time. Courtney could remember her coming to visit as a child, clutching Fluffy, her soft white albino cat with its odd pink eyes. Three days ago she'd arrived here with the sleek seal point Siamese that she'd acquired several years ago.

"What do you mean, not now?" Courtney asked, staring from her blue-eyed stepsister to the blue-eyed cat. "Is something wrong, Michelle?"

It was a question that she should have asked three days ago when Michelle and Burt had arrived for this unscheduled visit, Courtney acknowledged ruefully.

But things had been unusually hectic at work, and she'd been so preoccupied with her adoption story that she hadn't paused to wonder if there was a deeper reason for Michelle's impromptu visit other than she "had a few days off and felt like getting out of town."

Michelle caught her lower lip between her teeth. "Nothing's wrong, Courtney." She took a deep breath. "I've just been under a lot of pressure—at—at work, that's all."

She smiled, but Courtney noticed that her big, blue eyes were sad. Haunted, even.

"I thought you loved your job." Frowning, Courtney sat down on the high stool beside the counter. She couldn't remember Michelle ever complaining about her job as an administrative aide to a Pennsylvania state senator. Michelle had been an exceptional student who'd excelled all through school, and to no one's surprise, she excelled at her job, too.

"Oh, I do. But you know how it is—sometimes things get crazy." Michelle continued to pet the cat. "I really appreciate your letting me stay here for a few days, Courtney. It's great to just be away from—everything."

"You know you're welcome here anytime, Michelle," said Courtney, meaning it. The feeling that Michelle was hiding something was growing stronger by the minute. And then she remembered...if all went as planned in the Wilson Nollier interview tomorrow, she was supposed to leave for Shadyside Falls in the afternoon.

"Oh, Michelle!" she cried in dismay, and then launched into an explanation of the adoption story and her collaborative investigation with Connor McKay.

If Michelle was upset by the prospect of Courtney's

departure, she covered it masterfully. "I'm glad you're going to do something that might help Mark and Marianne get a baby. They want one so much, and they'll make terrific parents," she said, her blue eyes shining with sincerity. "And don't worry about me, Courtney. If you don't mind, Burton and I will stay here a couple more days before we head back. I'd love to do some sightseeing in the city. Aren't the cherry blossoms at their peak in April?"

Courtney's suspicions faded. She decided that she was feeling unnerved and anxious herself and had projected those feelings onto Michelle. "Stay as long as you like," she said warmly. "Although I don't recommend taking Burt on a tour of the White House. The First Dog might object."

"Burton doesn't do sightseeing, anyway. He'll be glad to sit here in the apartment and watch the birds from your kitchen window."

The cat meowed, as if in assent, and the two women laughed.

"Courtney, about this man who's going to pretend to be your husband," Michelle said carefully. "What's he like?"

"What's he like? Now there's a question!" Courtney's dark eyes flashed. "He's the most maddening, unfathomable man I've ever met. He makes me furious, but he makes me laugh, too. He's really smart, but sometimes he's so smart-alecky, I want to deck him."

"You?" Michelle looked astonished. "You've never decked anyone or anything in your entire life or ever wanted to—at least not as long as I've know you, and that's been since we were both four."

"I know, I know." Courtney threw up her hands. "But Connor McKay really gets to me."

"I see."

"No, no, I don't mean *that* way," Courtney hastened to assure her. "I mean, our—our personalities—clash. We're so different." And she was rapidly becoming inarticulate. She blushed.

Michelle surveyed her skeptically. "Opposites attract. And sometimes the chemistry can be explosive."

How well she knew! Courtney's blush deepened.

"You're attracted to him, aren't you?" Michelle pressed.

"I don't have to give in to it," Courtney insisted stubbornly. "As Daddy always says, we don't have to act on every thought or feeling that we have."

"That's vintage Carey philosophy." Michelle's voice trembled. "I used to be a fervent believer in it myself. I thought there were no feelings that couldn't be controlled with sufficient willpower."

She gave her head a quick shake, as if to clear it. "Be careful, Courtney. Even though Dad says it isn't possible, there are certain—forces that can bend even the strongest will. Sex is one of them. When the sex is good between them, a woman can become so vulnerable and dependent on the man that nothing, not willpower or common sense or anything else, can set her free. Sexual pleasure is such a powerful reward that a woman finds the man who gives it to her irresistible. So never, never get sexually hooked on a man who's wrong for you."

Courtney's eyes widened in concern. "Michelle, are you speaking from experience? Are you involved with a man who—"

"No! No, of course not! You mustn't take me literally, Courtney. I was merely quoting a magazine article I read recently. It seemed apt, if a bit melodramatic." Michelle flashed a smile so dazzling that Courtney had to blink.

Courtney gave her a measuring look. Michelle's dire words had chilled her. Was she really only quoting a magazine article? Carey family dogma held that the brilliant, organized and ever-perfect Michelle never had problems. Now Courtney wasn't so sure.

"Michelle, you know you can tell me anything and I'll do whatever I can to—"

"Courtney, I'm fine." Michelle reached for Courtney's hand and gave it an affectionate squeeze. "My little sis. You've always been so intense."

Courtney took her cue and dropped the subject of sex with the wrong man. Maybe Michelle really had been reading a magazine article. "*Little sis?*" she said lightly. "I'm only five months younger than you."

"That still makes you the baby of the family." Michelle gathered the cat into her arms and smiled again at Courtney. "I think Burton and I will turn in. I'll start making up the sofa bed."

"You can sleep with me in my room. I've got a double bed." Courtney made the offer she had been making since the first night Michelle arrived. "It'll be like old times. Remember how you used to share my room when you came to visit Daddy?"

Michelle nodded. "You were always so sweet and willing to share. I admit I was scared the first few times I came to visit after my dad married your mother. I mean, there you were, a little girl the same age as me living with your mother, sister, brother and *my* father and I was sure I'd been displaced."

Courtney shook her head. "Nothing would've made

your dad happier than to have had you and the other kids living with us full-time. I remember how sad he would be after the four of you left to go back to your mother's.''

"It's always hard to say goodbye," Michelle said softly. "And it never gets any easier. Nobody knows that better than we Careys."

"Wilson Nollier makes my skin crawl," Courtney said with a reminiscent shudder as she and Connor, in the front seat of his steel-gray Pontiac, drove along the interstate highway leading out of Washington, D.C., and heading west to the small West Virginia town of Shadyside Falls. "He was practically oozing that fake sympathy from every pore."

"You're one incredible actress, Gypsy. You played the part of the desperate wannabe-mommy to perfection."

Connor cast her a sidelong glance. The cheap imitation gold wedding band, which he had given to her prior to entering Nollier's office, was on her finger. She was still wearing the fawn-colored skirt and jacket she'd worn for the appointment. A deep-pink blouse added a splash of color to the outfit and he'd already noticed that as her emotions rose, her cheeks turned the shade of the blouse. She looked soft and sexy, and he didn't dare allow his gaze to drift to her sensually mobile mouth or her great dark eyes.

Connor shifted uncomfortably in his seat and tried to think of the business at hand. Wilson Nollier... Their appointment with the attorney earlier this afternoon in which they'd debuted in their roles as man and wife...Courtney had been astonishingly good. In fact, she'd been so convincing that he himself had come close to buying her story of childlessness.

"Have you studied drama or something?" he asked curiously.

Courtney shook her head no. "I've spent enough time with Mark and Marianne to know how much it hurts to want a baby and not have one." She shivered. "I hope that doesn't happen to me."

"You want kids?"

"Of course. Very much. Don't you?"

"I guess so." Connor shrugged. "I've never really thought about it."

He knew he was twisting the facts because he'd actually thought about it quite a bit. He liked children; he thoroughly enjoyed his sisters' kids. But when he tried to imagine having children of his own, he could never come close to conjuring up their mother, who would have to be—since he wasn't a completely untraditional guy—his wife.

And then there was the question of who his children would actually be? He was a McKay in name only; not by birth or even legal adoption. Did that make him a McKay by cash payment? And no matter what, he certainly couldn't lay claim to the exalted name of Tremaine, nor could any of his offspring. Would it be fair to inflict such a tainted, tangled legacy on an innocent child?

"Of course, it would be difficult to be much of a family man with the kind of job you have." Courtney cast a covert glance at him. He was even more attractive today in a blue-knit shirt that emphasized the rippling muscles of his shoulders and khaki slacks that hugged his flat belly and long muscular legs. She dragged her eyes away. "You probably don't keep regular hours. You're away a lot tracking down people who don't want to be tracked," she reminded herself aloud.

"Another one of your not-too-subtle swipes at my job, I presume?"

"I just think you should put your talents and your intelligence to good use instead of wasting them like you do."

Connor raised his brows. "What if I were to tell you that I worked my way through college and law school? That I passed the bar exam and am a licensed attorney in Virginia, Maryland and the District of Columbia?"

"What if I were to tell you that I'm the long-lost daughter of Elvis and Marilyn Monroe?" she retorted.

"I'd call Kaufman and tell him to inform his old pals at the *Globe Star Probe* to hold the presses." Connor laughed. "I get your point, Courtney. It is unbelievable that I could be anything other than a contemptible rebel without a cause."

Contemptible rebel without a cause. That's exactly what Connor McKay was; she couldn't have phrased it better herself. Then why did she feel this urge to deny it, to Connor and to herself?

Courtney shifted in her seat. It was time to turn this conversation away from the personal and back to business. "Do you think this rooming house where Wilson Nollier suggested we stay is under surveillance by his informers?"

"I think we can count on it. We can't let down our guard for a minute, Courtney. This Mrs. Mason, who runs the place, has got to believe we're a married couple who are desperate to adopt."

He swung the car onto the exit ramp, leaving the

wide smooth interstate for an older two-lane road. "According to the map, Shadyside Falls should be about an hour down this road."

"I'm starting to get nervous," Courtney confessed. "What if Nollier finds out what we're trying to do? Do you think he—" she paused and drew an anxious breath "—do you think he could be dangerous?"

"All cornered rats are dangerous, Gypsy. We'll just have to make sure he doesn't ever learn that we're cornering him." He turned up the radio. "Listen to some music. That'll calm your nerves."

It might have, if they couldn've found a station that played music. Unfortunately they were well into the countryside, and the only station they could pick up was airing a call-in talk show. The radio host was insulting and abusive, inciting his audience to respond with similar calls and threats.

Grimacing, Courtney switched it off. "We'll have to talk instead."

"You and I carry on a civil conversation? That can't last very long. Although we could consider it practice for the grueling ordeal ahead of us. And believe me, even *pretending* to be married is a grueling ordeal for me, Gypsy."

"Especially pretending to be married to me," Courtney concluded coolly. "Need I state the obvious? The feeling is entirely mutual."

Connor grinned. "Uh-oh, our civility is already starting to slide. Let's try another subject. Hmm, I've got one—your roommate. Does she work for NPB, too?"

"I don't have a roommate," said Courtney. "I live alone."

"Then who was the sexy-sounding babe who answered the phone last night when I called your place? The one who told me you were going to a party at Twin Oaks Country Club with Emery Harcourt.''

''Finding me really was a kindergarten exercise, wasn't it?'' Courtney smiled in spite of herself. ''You talked to my stepsister Michelle last night. She doesn't live with me, she lives in Harrisburg, but she and her cat are visiting me for a few days.''

''Stepsister? How's that? Your folks get divorced and remarry?''

''You ask a lot of questions,'' she complained mildly.

''Do you have any reasons for not wanting to answer them?''

''Pull your nasty fact-finding mind out of the gutter, Connor McKay. Not everyone has some deep, dark secret they want to hide.''

''You'd be surprised, Gypsy.''

''Well, I don't have any. Sorry to disappoint you.''

''Then why don't you want to talk about your family? Are you estranged from them?''

''Of course not!'' she spluttered. ''I love my family!''

''Yeah, I guess you must,'' he conceded. ''After all, you're letting your stepsister and stepcat stay with you, and you're willing to put up with playing the role of my wife to help Mark and Marianne find a baby.''

Courtney began to unbend a little. After all, his questions were innocuous enough, and it was going to be a long, boring drive if they rode the rest of the way in silence.

''My parents weren't divorced,'' she said. ''My father was killed in Vietnam two months before I was born. He was an army sergeant who saved two men by falling on a grenade and shielding them from it. He was awarded the Congressional Medal of Honor for heroism," she added proudly.

"So you grew up knowing about him, but never knowing him," Connor said thoughtfully. It strangely paralleled his own situation, except, of course, her real father had been a war hero, while his...

Connor's jaw tightened. His real father had been married to another woman when he'd irresponsibly knocked-up some little bimbo on the make and then bought his way out of the mess.

"I wish I'd known my father," Courtney said wistfully. "I've always been curious about him, wanting to know every little thing that anybody could remember. I did grow up with a dad, though," she added, her voice brightening. "My mother remarried when I was four, and my stepfather, John Carey, treated me like his own daughter. My older brother and sister, Mark and Ashlinn, and I have always used his last name and called him daddy. He had four kids by his first marriage, and they visited regularly with us. I was always closest to Michelle. Dad's an army major and retired five years ago to Florida with Mom. I grew up living on army posts all over the United States, West Germany and the Canal Zone, too. We moved every couple of years."

"You really *are* a gypsy. A lucky one. I spent my entire boring childhood and adolescence in the same crummy little Maryland town. As soon as I graduated from high school, I took off to hitchhike around the country to see what I'd been missing. A lot, it seemed."

"I think you were the lucky one," Courtney said softly. "I hated moving. I was heartbroken every time we left a place. I never felt like I had a hometown, and I wanted one. I wanted to really belong somewhere. I still do,'' she admitted.

"Ah, so that's the appeal Emery Harcourt holds for you? We all know it sure isn't sex appeal! Good old Emery is from a family with roots. The Harcourts have been living on the same plot of Virginia land since the eighteenth century, a land grant from the king, a fact that Sir Emery was quick to inform me last night. Those are mega-roots, to be sure, but to base a relationship on that is downright—''

"I don't want or need advice on relationships from someone who snoops and spies for a living and who views commitment as something akin to disease,'' Courtney interrupted indignantly.

"You don't approve of me at all, do you, Gypsy? It must really bug you that you heat up like a torch when I touch you, while the refined, well-rooted Emery leaves you cold. And don't try to deny that he doesn't. Not sleeping with a man you've dated for years is undeniable proof. If, God forbid, you and I were ever to *date,* we'd be in bed on the first one.''

Courtney jerked forward, mortified by his bald pronouncement. It was so unexpected. One moment, they'd actually been carrying on a civil conversation, and the next, he'd hit her with that red-hot memory of last night's interlude. She felt warm all over, remembering what she'd been determined to forget.

The man didn't play fair! She glared at him. "I won't even dignify that outrageous remark with a response.''

"Well done, Courtney. You sound as upper class as a born Harcourt or Tremaine.'' The sound of his family name on his lips unleashed a bolt of pain. And of all the feelings he disliked and avoided the most, pain topped the list. Anger was preferable. So Connor got angry.

As did Courtney. "I've never pretended to be upper class," she grated. "I'm an army brat who grew up in a family of seven kids and stepkids, where there was never enough money or enough room for everybody. I'm proud of my background, but I'm not ashamed of wanting something more, either."

"And you think you'll find it with Emery Harcourt?" argued Connor. "Good old rich, cultured, rooted-to-the-family-land Emery. Trust me on this one, Gypsy. Harcourt isn't what you're looking for."

"Well, it most certainly isn't *you!*" she burst out.

"Who said I was volunteering? I'm not interested in the position of Mr. Right, not for you or anyone else," he retorted scornfully, as if the idea of him wanting anything to do with her was positively ludicrous.

And she knew better. Last night she hadn't been the only one panting and throbbing in the passion of their embrace. Courtney was suddenly furious. She was sick and tired of him baiting her, setting her up for his sarcasm and then smirking loftily when she fell into his verbal traps.

"Aren't you?" she said, deliberately baiting *him.* "Don't bother to pretend that you don't want me, Connor. And it—it must really bug you that I prefer a sweet, gentle man like Emery to your tiresome macho posturing." She offered a silent apology to innocent, unsuspecting Emery for using him this way. Luckily he wouldn't find out.

"Oh, that's funny." But Connor wasn't laughing. "You prefer sweet, gentle Emery? Ha! I happened to

see the two of you sitting at that table when Kaufman
and I first arrived at the party. You were bored out of
your skull, Gypsy. I've seen people waiting in a dentist's office for a root canal look like they were having
a better time than you were having with the man of
your dreams.''

Where had he come up with that ''man of her
dreams'' stuff? Courtney fumed. Furthermore, his constant carping on her relationship with Emery Harcourt
was definitely getting old. It was terribly irritating to
have to keep up the pretense of herself and Emery as
a couple, but the more Connor dwelt on the subject,
the more she found it impossible to tell him the truth.

''I refuse to discuss the subject with you,'' she
snapped. ''In fact, I refuse to discuss any subject at
all with you. I'd rather listen to that idiot talk show
host and those atavistic imbeciles who call in and fight
with him than to waste my time talking to *you*.''

She switched on the radio. Connor immediately
turned it off.

''Fine.'' Courtney folded her arms and glared
straight ahead. ''It's your radio. If you don't want to
listen, we won't.''

They sat smoldering in silence as Connor followed
the roadside signs into Shadyside Falls. On the out-
skirts of town were a big discount mart, a convenience
store, a few gas stations and a rather seedy-looking
motel, each about a half mile from the other.

A set of railroad tracks literally divided the town in
half. Irregular rows of dilapidated wooden houses—
which were actually more like shacks—reminded
Courtney of the expression ''wrong side of the
tracks.'' The town square, built incongruously around
a circle, had a surprisingly bustling air. The bank,

beauty parlor, barber shop, a small hospital and several other stores were all open with people moving purposefully in and out conducting their business. The wide, clear window of Tell's Inn restaurant showed a capacity crowd. The boarded-up movie theater seemed to be the only building in town without customers.

"This isn't as bad as I was expecting," Courtney broke the silence to remark. "I mean, the people look normal, the town looks just like a small town anywhere."

"But of course. What were you expecting, a creepy, brooding place like one out of a Gothic novel or something?"

"Considering that children are bought and sold here, yes, I was expecting something sinister," Courtney retorted. "There's Ferrell's Market," she announced. "According to Nollier's directions, we're supposed to make a left at that corner and turn onto Maple Street. Mrs. Mason's house is number 26."

"Mrs. Mason on Maple Street. It sounds so homey and wholesome and all-American," observed Connor.

Courtney couldn't resist. "What were you expecting? The Log Lady on Murder Lane?"

Connor shot her a reluctant appreciative grin. "Could we call a cease-fire, beginning now, Gypsy? I don't think we should arrive at Mrs. Mason's place looking like archenemies."

"I agree. Although it probably wouldn't matter much if we did." Courtney grimaced. "All Wilson Nollier is interested in is the check for the baby. When he told us about the social worker who'll falsify the home study report for us, I almost choked. What he's saying is that he'll turn a baby over to anybody who has the cash regardless of their background or mental status or—or even morals."

It was a terrible realization and it made her doubly determined to end Nollier's racket.

Connor nodded grimly. He pulled the car in front of 26 Maple Street. The white frame house was two stories high with a big front porch and porticoes reminiscent of the Old South. The two of them stared at it for a moment. Then Connor extended his hand to Courtney.

"Let's put aside our own personal animosities to nail Nollier. Deal?"

"Deal." She put her hand in his for a firm shake.

"I do hope you'll be comfortable here," said the portly Mrs. Mason as she led Connor and Courtney up a narrow staircase and unlocked the door to one of the rooms lining a long, darkened hallway. "This is one of the very best rooms, just newly redecorated."

Courtney and Connor stepped inside and looked around. Though the entrance foyer and hallway were old and darkly shabby, this particular room had the ambience of a modern hotel room, right down to the color TV set on the dresser. The wallpaper, bold blue, white and green stripes, looked new, and there was a plush green carpet on the floor. An adjacent bathroom contained a double sink along with a shining tile shower stall.

No bathtub, Courtney noted, recalling her pledge to make Connor sleep in it. Her eyes returned to the queen-sized bed, the only bed in the room, with its spread that matched the wallpaper. She didn't dare look at Connor.

"Welcome to your temporary home away from

home," Mrs. Mason continued cheerily. "Just let me know what I can do to make your stay here as comfortable as possible. I like to keep my young parents relaxed and happy, and that means helping out with the little one, if need be. I've raised five of my own, so I don't panic easily. Mr. Nollier said the baby will be here within the hour. Oh, you must be over the moon with excitement."

Courtney's jaw dropped. The bed problem was instantly relegated to back-burner status. "The baby?" she managed to say.

"What baby?" asked Connor.

"Why, *your* new baby, of course!" exclaimed Mrs. Mason. She opened a door to what Courtney had assumed was a closet. It wasn't. "Here's the baby's room, connecting to yours." The room was small, with a crib and changing table almost filling it.

For a full minute, Courtney and Connor stood stock-still, stunned into speechlessness. Finally Courtney rallied herself to repeat incredulously, "The baby is coming today? *In an hour?*"

Mrs. Mason nodded. "I expect you and your husband will want to head on out to the drugstore and pick up diapers and baby formula and clothes, of course. Not that a newborn baby needs to be a fashion-plate, mind you," she added, rather sternly. "I don't see spending a fortune on baby clothes that an infant will outgrow in a matter of weeks. Why, the prices these days—"

"Wilson Nollier told us to stay here to wait for a baby," Connor cut into what promised to be a splendidly economic diatribe. "He didn't say it would be today!"

He still couldn't believe it. From the facts he'd gathered on adoption, babies were elusive; couples waited years for an infant to come their way. Yet he and Courtney had just placed their order, so to speak, a few hours earlier, and now delivery was imminent? From the dumbfounded expression on Courtney's face, it was obvious that she was feeling equally confused.

"Babies have a way of coming when it suits them," Mrs. Mason chuckled knowingly. "Now, you two run along and buy those supplies. I'll have sheets on the bed and the crib by the time you get back."

Courtney stood rooted to the spot. "Is—is there a phone? I think we ought to call Mr. Nollier and talk to him about this."

"He'll be here soon. He's the one bringing the baby—who'll need formula and diapers," Mrs. Mason added with a note of exasperated impatience.

Courtney ran her hand through her dark hair, tousling it. She felt as if she'd wandered into a play well into the third act and was somehow supposed to instantly pick up the threads of the plot. Her eyes met Connor's. He looked exactly the way she felt.

"What are you going to name her?" Mrs. Mason asked chattily. She linked one arm through Courtney's and the other through Connor's and briskly walked the stunned couple out of the room and back down the stairs.

"Her?" Connor echoed. He sounded shockingly stupid, even to his own ears.

"Your new little daughter. Oh, gracious, didn't I mention that your baby was a girl?" Mrs. Mason chortled with self-mocking humor. "Well, she is. A darling little girl. Three days old and perfect in every way, according to Mr. Nollier. What a nice little family you'll be."

Six

"**A** nice little family!" Connor repeated for the third time as he and Courtney drove back through town toward the drugstore. "You, me and the baby." He looked as dazed as he sounded.

"What are we going to do?" cried Courtney. She was trying hard not to panic, but wasn't having much success. "Connor, we didn't get one incriminating bit of evidence on Nollier from the interview in his office this afternoon, except that statement about the social worker 'fixing' the home study, and he could easily claim it was an innocent remark, slang for simply getting the study done."

"I know, I know." Connor strove to stay calm. It wasn't easy. "We were supposed to be here awhile, keep our eyes and ears open, ask questions and try to gather some evidence. Instead, we're here all of ten minutes and suddenly we're on our way to buy diapers.''

"The plan was to get Nollier on tape demanding a huge sum of money from us and then turning us down when we couldn't come up with it. Instead we're getting a baby!'' Courtney's voice rose. "Connor, we aren't even married!''

"Try not to get upset. If we lose our cool, we're finished,'' Connor said with more conviction than he felt. The truth was, his own cool had evaporated the moment jolly Mrs. Mason informed him that he and Courtney were about to become parents. "Let's take a few minutes and try to think this through.''

"All I can think is that I don't know what kind of baby formula to buy,'' moaned Courtney. "I know how to take care of a baby, but I don't know a thing about formula and bottles. My older stepsister, Cathy, has three kids, and my two stepbrothers have two each, but all three mothers breast-fed their babies, so I never dealt with bottles and formula. Connor, what are we going to do?''

"We're going to do what we planned—only a lot sooner,'' Connor said with sudden conviction. "When Nollier arrives with the baby, he'll have to ask for the money, won't he? When he tells us the sum, we'll say we can't afford it. We'll keep him talking, get him to admit that he won't give us the baby because we can't meet his price. That's definite baby-selling, Gypsy. Incriminating as hell.''

He swung the car into the large parking lot of the drugstore.

"If we don't give Nollier the cash, he'll take the baby away,'' Courtney said gloomily. "We don't actually have to buy anything here.''

"But we can't come back to the house empty-handed. Mrs. Mason will get suspicious. After all, we're not supposed to know that we can't finance this child. We'll save the receipts and return all the stuff we buy here tomorrow."

They went to the baby department and, with the aid of a helpful clerk, bought several cans of a quality-brand formula, a selection of bottles, diapers, little white undershirts and several soft pastel stretch suits. On impulse, Courtney put a tiny smocked pink dress and pink knit booties into the cart.

"I want her to keep the dress," she said, staring at the delicate little garment with troubled dark eyes. "Nollier can give it to the person he sells her to."

The very thought made her blood run cold. It was one thing to talk about selling babies in the abstract, but when it came to being given the opportunity to buy a child herself, the situation was almost beyond comprehension. Tears filled her eyes, and she frantically blinked them back as they stood in the checkout line.

"Connor, suppose Wilson Nollier sells the baby to terrible people who'll mistreat her and hurt her?" she whispered hoarsely. "It'll be all our fault because we gave her back to Nollier instead of—"

"Buying her ourselves?" Connor hissed in a whisper. "Adopting her? Courtney, that's not an option, for God sake! As you pointed out in the car, we're not married. We can't keep the baby!"

"Then let's pay his price and give her to Mark and Marianne," cried Courtney. "Oh, please, Connor! We—"

"Get a grip, Courtney. If we bought the baby, we'd be perpetrating the very crime we're supposed to be investigating." He pulled a handkerchief from the pocket of his slacks and wiped his perspiring brow. "What a partner you turned out to be! You fall apart in the first moments of our first case!"

She bit her lip. "I'm sorry," she murmured. "You're right."

She sounded so woebegone that Connor's usually hardened heart went out to her. He placed his hand over hers as she pushed the cart forward. "Keeping Nollier from placing babies in the hands of the highest cash bidders is why we're doing this, Courtney. And don't worry, we'll see to it that the baby girl isn't placed with terrible people."

"Don't try to placate me," she snapped in a low voice, jerking her hand out from under his. "You know as well as I do that we'll never know what happens to that child once Nollier takes her away. There is no way we can possibly prevent him from selling the baby to whomever he wants."

"You don't have to bite my head off!" Connor was miffed. The one time he'd impulsively tried to be soothing instead of sarcastic and she'd flung the words back at him. "I was only trying to—"

"Trivialize the fate of that baby! Detach yourself from it and her and trying to get me to do the same. Well, I won't, Connor McKay. Unlike you, I'm not afraid to make commitments and keep them. And we—"

"We're next," he interrupted coldly, feeling undeservedly misunderstood. "Start unloading the cart."

They weren't speaking as they cleared the checkout line and carried their purchases back to the car. Nor did they exchange a single word until they were back in their room at Mrs. Mason's house, surrounded by their luggage and packages.

"Unbutton your blouse," Connor ordered.

Her heart slammed against the wall of her chest. "What?" She was suddenly very aware that they were alone together—in a bedroom. And that she really didn't know him very well at all.

Connor glanced at her pale face and anxious brown eyes. "Oh, for godsakes, I'm not going to assault you." He made an exclamation of disgust. "I want to put a wire on you—for Nollier's visit. Wilson Nollier, remember him? The reason why you and I are here?"

"I can do without the sarcasm, thank you." Courtney sniffed. "Violence is so pervasive these days, women can't help being paranoid. Anyway, why don't you wear the wire?"

"Because you'd have to tape it to me and I don't trust you to do the job right. Anyway, that tape sticks to the hair on my chest and it's excruciating to pull off. I can fasten the wire to your bra," he added, narrowing his eyes. "You do wear one, don't you? I can't tell with that flak jacket you're wearing."

Courtney spluttered, flustered. To which of his well-aimed attacks should she respond first? That her stylish jacket no way resembled a flak jacket in any shape or form? That she did indeed wear a bra—but if he thought she was going to unbutton her blouse for him, he was definitely delusional. And then there was his remark about his chest. She'd already ogled the muscular strength of him; now her mind mentally added a thick mat of wiry-soft hair to that broad masculine expanse.

While she was dealing with all of this, Connor took action. He began to unbutton her blouse with the deft expertise of one who has completed the task many times.

"Stop!" Courtney slapped at his hands. "I refuse to let—"

"Relax, Gypsy." Connor smiled that caustic smile she loathed. "I'm not trying to seduce you, either. And I promise that the sight of your bra isn't going to thrust me into the throes of foaming lust. I just want to clip the wire onto you, not cop a feel. Now stand still."

Courtney's cheeks burned. His fingers were brushing against the softness of her breasts as he reached into the cup of her bra to attach the wire. She felt her nipples growing taut as they strained against the lace. If the tip of his index finger were to move just a centimeter or two lower, he would be touching the sensitive aureole.

Nor was Connor as unaffected as he pretended by the intimacy. Her skin was smooth as satin to the touch, and he had to look at her in order to properly adjust the wire. What he saw was a lacy pink bra, and he couldn't help wondering if she was wearing matching panties, tiny sexy ones, the kind that clouded a man's mind on sight. Filling the cups of that ultra-feminine bra were full and rounded milk-white breasts, which were paradoxically both soft and firm and so tantalizing that desire, sharp and swift, sliced through him.

His breathing quickened and he fumbled with the clip. It fell deeper into the cup and he reached for it, brushing her nipple as he retrieved it. Courtney gasped. The brief touch sent a lightning bolt of sensation all the way to her most secret, intimate parts.

Connor felt the tight hard bud and a sensual heaviness pooled in his groin in response. He couldn't help himself, he had to touch her again. Deliberately this time, he dropped the clip, then sent his fingers onto a search mission inside the cup of her bra.

Courtney sucked in her breath. A wildly pleasurable tightness spiraled through her as his hand moved against her. His fingers were moving slowly as they gently probed her nipple, which was growing even harder and more sensitive. She had never experienced anything as electrifying as the delicious feelings that surged through her as he stroked and caressed her with his clever hand.

Courtney heard a soft little sound escape from the back of her throat, and she arched her spine so that her breast pressed boldly into his palm. Her knees felt weak; it was difficult to hold her eyelids open. She wanted to close them, to lie down and...

Connor gave up the phony quest for the clip along with any attempt to wire her. Gathering evidence was the last thing on his mind as the tantalizing scent of her perfume filled his nostrils. His fingers were trembling with anticipation and need as he unfastened the front clasp on her bra, but he was too aroused to worry about the absence of his characteristic laconic cool. Her bra fell away, and when his hands fully cupped her breasts, both Courtney and Connor sighed.

"Oh God, Gypsy," he whispered, his lips feathering her temple and her sleek, dark hair. "You're so soft, so sweet." His hands slid to her waist and he guided her to the bed which stood a convenient half-foot away.

Swiftly he pulled her down on it, lying beside her so they were face-to-face.

The change in position, from vertical to horizontal, enabled Courtney to briefly surface from the sensual quicksand enveloping her. "Connor," she murmured, shivering as his mouth trailed down the sensitive curve of her neck. His hands were back on her breasts, fondling, squeezing, making her ache with a hunger she had never known.

"We can't," she whispered on a moan. But as if of their own volition, her hands slid along the length of his arms to rest on his shoulders. The supple strength of him distracted her. She flexed her fingers, feeling his muscles ripple beneath her touch. Suddenly the cotton shirt he wore was a frustrating barrier.

"We—we shouldn't," she amended breathlessly.

"I know," Connor grated in reply. His mouth was open and hot against hers. "I know."

He thrust his tongue into her mouth without any idle preliminaries, his hunger too great to indulge in his usual premeditated foreplay. Desire, urgent and heavy, tightened his body.

Courtney melted against him, the softness of her body accommodating itself to the hard masculine planes of his. With a sensual groan, Connor deepened the kiss, demanding and receiving an intimately passionate response that she gave willingly and without reservation.

Her senses were reeling, her body warm and arching into his. The sparks that had been kindled during those previous, aborted kisses blazed to full intensity, burning away all inhibitions and thoughts of resistance. Courtney clung to him, dizzy with the unfamiliar but irresistible pleasure and desire he was rousing in her. She wanted it to go on and on.

Connor's breathing was hard and fast and his hands moved over her, learning the shape of her, all the feminine curves and hollows concealed by her modestly cut suit—which he wanted to strip off her so he could savor the feel of her bare skin.

He felt as if he were going a little crazy. Never had he burned like this, not even in the heady randy days of adolescence. He dimly recognized that if he were in full control of his faculties, he would be pulling back, unable and unwilling to accept the power this woman had over him. He was used to being the master of his passions, he never lost his head, yet he was coming dangerously close to doing exactly that.

But none of that seemed to matter now.

Cradling Courtney in his arms, Connor rolled her onto her back, coming down on top of her. She relished the intoxicating heaviness of his weight, wrapping her arms around him and wriggling sensuously beneath him.

"I said I wasn't going to seduce you," Connor rasped, his head spinning, as if he'd had one too many shots of one-hundred-proof bourbon. "But, baby, I think you're seducing me!"

He slipped his leg between hers, forcing her narrow skirt to hike up high on her thighs. Connor glided his hand along the long, smooth length of her leg, encased in sheer rose-tinted stockings. Courtney's toes curled in her shoes and her leather pumps dropped off her feet, one by one. Her body arched into his and she felt his virile hardness pressing intimately against her. This shouldn't be happening, she thought vaguely, dazedly. It was too fast, too soon and...

"Never, never get sexually hooked on a man who is wrong for you." Michelle's words flashed to mind but were quickly submerged in the warm seas of sensuality into which she was slipping. When Connor claimed her mouth for another deep, hungry kiss, her

eyes closed in ecstasy and she gave into the pure primal pleasure of it.

It took several long moments for the sharp, staccato knocks on the door to penetrate the passionate mists enveloping them. Slowly, dazedly, they drew apart and sat up, staring at each other with slumberous, heavy-lidded eyes.

"Mr. Nollier is here with the baby," Mrs. Mason called through the closed door. "I told him you'd be right down."

Connor inhaled sharply. Courtney covered her cheeks with her hands. The baby!

"We'll be right there," Connor said. His voice was husky and thick and the sensuous sound of it sent a shudder of response through Courtney.

"Connor," she whispered, laying her hand on his thigh. She remembered that old pop standard her mother sometimes played. "Bewitched, Bothered and Bewildered." She'd thought the title effectively alliterative, but now she fully appreciated the sentiments behind the words. It was the way she was feeling now.

Mrs. Mason's urgent announcement took second place to the restlessness that churned through her. Her mind was filled with Connor. He'd been so tender with her, so hungry for her. And she had never responded to a man with such passion in her life. Her body still felt heavy and liquid and deliciously, languidly sensual.

Despite the timing and the crucial events about to unfold, she craved his touch. Even a smile or a kind word would suffice, anything to let her know that what had just happened between them meant something to him. That she meant something more to him than merely a physical way to pass some time.

Connor stood up, making a few necessary adjustments to his clothing. "We've got to go down now," he said tonelessly, heading toward the door. He didn't look back at her. He didn't trust himself to continue walking away from her were he to glimpse her kiss-swollen mouth or her soft, exposed breasts.

Courtney blushed scarlet and she tried not to show the hurt she felt at his abrupt dismissal. As she fumbled with the front-fastening clasp of her bra with trembling fingers, she spied the forgotten clip, which had fallen to the carpet. "What about the wire?" she murmured.

Connor heaved an impatient groan. "Can you do it yourself?"

"No, I don't know how to. I normally don't lead the kind of life that requires secret wires and taping," she added defensively.

Connor said nothing at all as he attached the clip to her brassiere, and he moved away from her with precision speed to set up the recording equipment. Both were very careful to avoid each other's eyes. "I'll wait for you on the stairs," he said brusquely. He had to get away from her or he would pull her back into his arms!

Courtney finished buttoning her blouse, then quickly glanced in the mirror as she ran a brush through her hair. Her cheeks were the same rosy color as her blouse, her lips were sensitive and slightly swollen, the lipstick completely gone. Reflexively she touched her fingertips to her mouth, remembering the feel of Connor's lips, of his tongue....

She bolted from the room, determined to put the memory away as abruptly and thoroughly as Connor had.

They entered Mrs. Mason's sunny living room, where she stood cooing over the pink-and-white bundle that Wilson Nollier held in the crook of his arm.

"Ah, Connor, Courtney," the attorney greeted them with his usual unctuous friendliness. "Here she is. Your daughter." Beaming, he placed the sleeping infant in Courtney's arms.

Courtney stared down at the tiny infant, who had a shock of straight, silky, coal-black hair. One small hand was curved over the edge of the blanket, the incredibly delicate little fingers balled into a fist. "She's the prettiest baby I've ever seen," she whispered.

Courtney gazed raptly at the baby in her arms, her eyes drinking in each and every infant feature—the rosebud mouth, the amazingly small but perfectly arched eyebrows, the dainty shell of an ear. "Oh, she's precious!"

"And she's your little girl," Wilson Nollier said smoothly. He draped his arm around Mrs. Mason's plump shoulders. "Seeing a mother meet her child for the first time is one of the most beautiful sights in the world, isn't it, June?"

The older woman dabbed her eyes with a handkerchief. "One I'll never tire of seeing, Mr. Nollier."

Connor wanted to gag. The hypocrisy of those two pirates nauseated him. He knew damn well that the sizable check the baby brought in was the most beautiful sight in the world to Nollier, and Mrs. Mason undoubtedly never tired of receiving her payoff for whatever part she played in this racket. What if he and Courtney really were the baby-hungry couple that they'd presented themselves to be? Having handed the child to the hopeful adoptive mother, Nollier would not hesitate to rip it from her arms if the cash payment wasn't large enough. What smarmy comments did he have in stock for that heartbreaking moment? Connor wondered cynically.

"Oh, Connor, look! She's opened her eyes!" Courtney cried excitedly. "They're blue!" She stared in fascination as the baby looked up at her with big, wide-set blue eyes. Courtney felt an instant shock of recognition. "Sarah!" she said softly.

A rush of sweet memories rolled through her mind as she remembered that Christmas morning when she'd found Sarah, a life-sized vinyl baby doll with blue eyes and black rooted hair under the tree. It had been the first Christmas after their mother had married John Carey, and even now, Courtney could recall the warmth and security and happiness of that day. She was four years old and all her wishes had come true—she had a daddy and the baby doll she wanted. Sarah promptly became her most prized possession and went everywhere with her. The doll had been all over the world with her and now resided comfortably, wrapped in a cotton pillowcase, on the top shelf of her bedroom closet.

Smiling, Courtney gazed down into the alert blue eyes of this new little Sarah. She felt the same kind of instant bond, of shared destiny she'd felt that magical Christmas morning. The baby was staring up at her with innocence and trust, and a sudden fierceness, staggering in its intensity, left Courtney nearly breathless. She knew in that moment that she was never going to give this child back to Wilson Nollier.

Connor's eyes were drawn again and again to Courtney and the baby. The two of them looked so natural together, so right. Even their hair color matched! Courtney had mentioned that she had nieces and nephews, and it was obvious she knew a thing or two about babies. She certainly looked at ease holding the infant in her arms.

At ease? taunted a voice in his head. There was so much more to the image than that. She looked beautiful, her eyes tender, her smile loving and warm as the baby's gaze connected with hers. Connor stared at the pair, transfixed.

"Mrs. Mason tells me you've settled in, Connor," Wilson Nollier's voice broke the silence that had fallen over the room. "Do you have everything you need?"

The bastard actually sounded solicitous, Connor thought, and a sudden wave of fury coursed through him. He decided he couldn't endure any more of Nollier's slick smoothness. It was time to put an end to this little drama, to nail Nollier once and for all.

"You didn't name a price in the office this afternoon," Connor said, moving to stand closer to Courtney, hoping to lure Nollier closer as well. They needed him within audio range to get his voice clearly on tape. "Of course, we never expected to—uh—get a baby so soon and—"

"Connor, please, let's not talk about it right now," Courtney interrupted, looking up at him with pleading dark eyes. She was filled with dread as she clutched the baby closer.

Nollier smiled. "I agree with your wife, Connor. This is no time to talk about money. Hold your daughter. Get to know her!"

Sink the hook in deeper, Connor translated bitterly. Get to know the child so that money would be no object when it came to keeping her. So that was the subtle way this baby-broker manipulated the hearts, minds—and cash resources—of his defenseless clients? He mentally called Nollier every obscene name he'd ever heard.

"I'm a man who insists on paying my bills promptly," Connor said, hoping that he'd managed to keep the disgust he felt for the attorney from his tone, from his eyes. "What do we owe you, Mr. Nollier?"

"I'll just go into the kitchen and put on a pot of coffee," Mrs. Mason said quickly. "I have homemade coconut cake, too, my own dear grandmother's recipe." The woman bustled from the room.

Connor watched her absent herself from the proceedings with a sardonic eye. Coffee and cake added such a nice homey touch to the impersonal business of child-selling.

"I have the mother's hospital bill right here." Nollier reached inside the pocket of his suitcase and pulled out a form. "The receipt, that is. The bill has already been paid in full by my firm." He handed the paper to Connor. "The client reimburses us."

Connor stared at it. The top of the bill read Shadyside Falls Hospital, and it looked legitimate, an itemized account of a three-day hospital stay, including delivery room suite fee, doctor's expenses, meals and pain relievers. The price was high, but not out of line; in fact, he knew for a fact that costs in the Washington area hospitals were substantially higher.

"Can you afford to pay it, Connor?" Nollier asked. The concern in his voice sounded astonishingly authentic. "You don't have to pay it all at once, you know, I can arrange for a monthly installment plan. And if you can't swing that, well then, just pay me whatever you feel you can afford without jeopardizing your financial status."

Connor was certain he hadn't heard right. He couldn't have. Paying a mother's hospital bill was perfectly legal in private adoption, and this bill had not been padded in any way.

He looked at Courtney, who was staring at Nollier, her face mirroring her own confusion.

"What about your fee and the—uh—legal expenses?" she asked reluctantly. Here it comes, she thought anxiously. An astronomical fee that Connor will have to decline to pay. And then Nollier will demand Sarah back and—and he couldn't have her!

Wilson Nollier smiled, showing his even white teeth. "I'm waiving my fee, Courtney, and that includes all legal costs. My firm can absorb them."

She was flummoxed. "But—but why?"

Nollier's smile widened. "You and Connor are a fine, generous young couple who want to share your life with a child. This little girl needs a home. The woman who gave birth to her is a college student, just twenty-one years old and unmarried. Unfortunately the baby's father, a professor at the same college, is already married and ended the affair as soon as he learned there was to be a child. The mother is a bright, concerned young woman who wants the best for her baby. I think you and Connor are that, Courtney—the best. It's my pleasure to bring the three of you together. Money is irrelevant."

He sounded so sincere. And what he'd said was beautiful. Courtney felt emotional tears fill her eyes. Could she and Connor somehow have been terribly wrong about Wilson Nollier?

I hope we got that heartwarming speech on tape,

Connor thought irritably, as a cynical smile curved his lips. It was obvious that somehow, someway, Wilson Nollier had gotten word of who they were and their plans to set him up. Instead, he had set *them* up, spouting a completely unincriminating—even inspirational!—message for their tape. What a cool, smooth operator the man was! If he didn't despise him so much, Connor decided that he would have to admire the attorney's aplomb.

Well, he had nothing to lose, so he may as well go for broke. Perhaps he could anger Nollier into giving something away. "You're not known for your generosity in this business, Mr. Nollier. Tell me the real reason why you're suddenly so altruistic?"

Courtney stood up, cradling the baby against her. "If you'll excuse me," she said anxiously, wanting to get away from the confrontation she knew was coming. "I'd like to take the baby upstairs."

She waited expectantly for Nollier to order her to stop, to demand that the baby be kept in his sight. But it was Connor who held out a restraining hand. "Stay here, Courtney," he commanded.

"Let her go," Wilson Nollier interjected. "You don't trust me, do you, Connor? Astute of you. I'd be skeptical in these circumstances myself."

Connor scowled. "What kind of game are you playing, Nollier?"

"Courtney, my dear, run along. Take the baby up to your room, if you wish," Nollier said, dismissing her as if she were a child being sent off to play.

Courtney was too grateful to escape with Sarah to object. She hurried from the room, the small pink bundle tucked safely in her arms. She was on the first step when she changed her mind and crept back to stand in the shadows of the hall, directly outside the living room. She owed it to Connor—and to baby Sarah—to stay. Having two witnesses to whatever Nollier was about to say would double their credibility.

Alone in the living room, Connor turned cold green eyes on the attorney. He suspected that Nollier had guessed Courtney was wearing a wire, thus his eagerness to dispatch her out of range. But why had Courtney gone? His lips tightened. Whose side was she on, anyway?

"Okay, Nollier. Courtney's not here. Are you going to level with me?" More than likely, the weasel would laugh at him and their overconfident, amateur plan.

But Wilson Nollier wasn't laughing; his expression was one of approval. "You're neither stupid nor naive, Connor," he said, and his tone was approving, too. "But then, I wouldn't expect a son of Richard Tremaine's to be. You're sharp, just like the rest of the Tremaines."

Seven

Outside in the hall, Courtney stood rigid and stunned. *Richard Tremaine was Connor's father?* She inched closer to the threshold, wishing she could see Connor's face. Was it true? Did he know?

"Your real father is Richard Tremaine, Connor," Wilson Nollier said quietly. "I think you should have been told the truth years ago, but since you weren't, I feel that I owe it to you to tell you now."

Courtney remembered the tension that had gripped Connor when he'd pointed out Richard Tremaine to her at the club. Suddenly she was certain that Connor was already aware of his true parentage.

Connor verified it. "I've known Richard Tremaine was my father since my thirteenth birthday. My—foster father told me the whole story of my origins."

"He did?" Nollier frowned. "You mean you've known all these years?"

Connor shrugged. "Sure."

"Exactly what did McKay tell you?" Nollier pressed. "I never did trust that man. Dennis McKay was too ingratiating, too eager to please. My own gut feeling was that McKay harbored a lot of hostility that could end up hurting you and your mother. I tried at the time to tell Richard—"

"Oh, give me a break, Nollier!" Connor actually laughed. The thought of Wilson Nollier earnestly advising Richard Tremaine not to pay the McKays to take his unwanted son struck him as patently absurd. Nollier undoubtedly had handled the deal, with generous com- pensation for his work. But who would've expected the attorney to connect his name to that long-ago deal? Connor thought ruefully. After all, thirty-four years had passed, along with countless other cases. Nollier's memory was superb!

"Connor, you're the son of one of my oldest friends. I've known about your existence since the day you were born—and even before that! I'll never forget the night Richard came to tell me that your mother was pregnant." Nollier removed a handkerchief from his suit coat and swiped it over his brow.

"That must've been quite a night," Connor said sarcastically.

"Oh, it was." Nollier took a deep breath. "But I lost track of you over the years. I wasn't even aware that you'd married. When my secretary gave me your name to set up an appointment, I recognized it instantly. Why do you think I agreed to see you immediately? And when you walked into my office this afternoon with your wife, I was shaken to the core! You look so much like your father did at your age. And your resemblance to young Tyler, your half-brother, is unmistakable. Different coloring, but the features are the same."

Courtney angled her position to enable her to look inside the living room. She watched Connor drop onto the overstuffed sofa, his green eyes haunted. The baby made a tiny mewing sound, and she gazed down to see the infant studying her intently, as if trying to divine exactly what was going on.

Courtney touched her lips against Sarah's soft downy cheek. She thought of the young woman who had given birth to this baby, who believed her child would be raised in a loving, secure home. *She will,* Courtney silently promised the unknown birth mother. *I'm Sarah's mother now, and I'll always love and protect her.*

In the living room, Connor was staring hard at Nollier. "I don't know why, but I think I believe you." He was burning with questions. About Richard Tremaine, about his birth mother. Was she really the callous, amoral slut Dennis McKay had hinted that she was?

"I have no reason to lie to you," Nollier said quietly. He glanced at his watch, a diamond-studded Rolex. "If you ever want to know the full story of your father and mother, which I'll wager is quite different from the version McKay gave you, I'll be glad to tell you everything I know. But, unfortunately, not now. I have to get back to the city for another appointment. Tell Mrs. Mason I'm sorry to miss her incomparable cake and coffee."

"Nollier, why did you tell me all this?" Connor demanded, blocking his way.

"Because I want you to know why I'm willing to foot the bill for the entire adoption, if need be," said

Nollier. "You're Richard's son and I've always felt you got one helluva bum deal in life. When your wife told me the problems you've had trying to have a baby, then trying to adopt, I made up my mind to help you anyway I could. I didn't want you to have to wait another day for a child, I wanted an *immediate* happy ending for you. Now there is one, at last. You have a sweetheart of a wife and a healthy new baby."

He gave Connor's shoulder an avuncular pat. "Why don't you let me do one more thing and arrange a meeting with your father? Your real father, Richard Tremaine. It's time you two met. I know how much he would—"

"No." Connor shook his head. "Absolutely not."

Nollier sighed. "You're more like him than you know. Cautious, controlled, willing to wait—until the golden moment to act is long past. But it's your choice, Connor. I won't pressure you—now. About the baby…"

Courtney walked into the living room, the baby in her arms. She would *not* allow Connor to give Sarah back to the attorney, even though their plan had collapsed.

"Ah, here is the lovely Courtney," Nollier said smoothly as she entered. "I was just about to tell your husband that it will be necessary for you two to remain here in Shadyside Falls for at least a couple weeks with the baby while the adoption paperwork is being processed."

"Why?" demanded Connor.

"It serves an archaic state residency requirement." Nollier rolled his eyes heavenward. "I have extremely able people working for me, and we've managed to

cut the ridiculous waiting periods required by tenacious bureaucrats—''

"How do you manage that?'' Connor interrupted.
"Bribery?''

Nollier smiled. "You even have your father's droll
sense of humor, I see. To continue,'' he went on
smoothly, "my colleagues in the human services office cannot be persuaded to completely eliminate the
residency requirement, even though it's been drasti-
cally curtailed. My personal opinion is that these particular persons—originally Shadyside Falls natives—
like the revenue the adoptive parents pour into the
town during their stay here.''

"I'll bet,'' Connor muttered, wondering how many
others in the town ran profitable "homes-away-from
home'' like the accommodating Mrs. Mason.

Nollier shrugged. "However, our couples don't find
the wait a great hardship. They spend a few carefree
weeks here and leave with their child, the adoption
legal and permanent.''

Mrs. Mason entered the living room carrying a wide
silver tray loaded with cups of coffee and thick slices
of cake.

"So sorry. I must run.'' Wilson Nollier snatched his
attaché case and was out of the room before anyone
could utter a protest.

"Always in such a hurry,'' Mrs. Mason grumbled
reprovingly. "Won't you two sit down and—''

The baby opened her eyes and let out a small but
unmistakable wail. "She might be wet or hungry,''
Courtney said quickly. "Or maybe both. I'll take her
upstairs.'' She disappeared from the room even faster
than Wilson Nollier had.

"To be honest with you, Mrs. Mason, I couldn't eat

a piece of cake if my life depended on it." Connor was the next to head out of the room.

Mrs. Mason watched him leave, then shrugged, sat down and dug her fork into the first piece of cake.

Connor watched Courtney change the baby's diaper, then sit down on the bed and settle the infant in her arms with a bottle of milky-looking formula.

"We're not staying, Gypsy. As soon as the baby is fed, you can hand her over to Mrs. Mason. We've blown our chance to nail Nollier, at least in this particular case, so there is no reason for us to hang around here."

"*I'm* staying," Courtney countered firmly. "I want to legally adopt Sarah."

"Have you lost your mind?" Connor gasped. "You can't adopt a baby!"

"Why not? Single people adopt all the time these days. I have enough money in my bank account to pay Nollier for the hospital expenses, I have a job and can support a child, and I'm confident I can be a good mother to my little Sarah." She gazed down at the baby who was sucking the nipple greedily. A flood of maternal warmth filled her.

"Your little Sarah? You really have flipped! Courtney, have you forgotten why we came here in the first place? We—"

"I haven't forgotten. The documentary will be made. True, there is nothing on the record we can use pertaining to Wilson Nollier, but we won't have that information, anyway, no matter if we go or stay."

"What about your brother and his wife?" Connor injected shrewdly. "How are Mark and Marianne going to feel when you waltz back to Washington with the baby you've adopted? They've been trying for years to adopt with no luck and then you find a child in one day!''

Courtney winced. He'd fired an effective volley there. She tried to think logically, not react emotionally. "It's not as if Nollier will let Mark and Marianne adopt her. You know he won't. The only reason why he gave us Sarah in the first place is because you're—'' she broke off abruptly.

"I'm what?'' demanded Connor.

Courtney sighed. "I may as well admit it. I was eavesdropping the entire time, Connor. I know you're Richard Tremaine's son.''

"Oh, great!'' Connor sank down onto the bed beside her. Resting his elbows on his knees, he held his head in his hands. "Just great.''

"Don't worry. I swear I won't ever tell a soul.''

"I wasn't worried that you'd hightail it to a phone and pass along the news to Kieran Kaufman.'' Connor grimaced. "But I never wanted anyone else to know—'' He halted in midsentence.

"This is one of those dramatic moments of truth,'' Courtney said quietly. "You suddenly comprehend the kind of pain and embarrassment that your *fact-finding* has unleashed in other people's lives. It could happen to you and to the Tremaines if some opportunistic snoop learns the truth.''

He felt winded, as if he'd been kicked in the stomach. But admitting vulnerability—especially to a woman, especially to *her*—was anathema to him. He stood up and swaggered around the room a bit.

"What do I care if some cretin like Kaufman finds out I'm a Tremaine—how does that quaint euphemism for bastard go?—born on the wrong side of the blanket? Actually it would enhance my own position. Think of all those sexy little fortune-hunters who'd chase me, hoping for a cut of the Tremaine loot. As for Richard Tremaine and his sons, well—''

"Connor, you can skip the hard-as-nails tough-guy act," Courtney cut in sternly. "I'm not buying it. You care very much. If you'd wanted to hurt or embarrass the Tremaines you would have done it years ago. You don't want the notoriety yourself, either."

She gently lifted Sarah to her shoulder and rubbed her small back until the baby emitted a loud burp. The infant's big, blue eyes widened in surprise at the sound. Courtney laughed in delight.

Connor turned to stare at the baby. "She belched like a drunken sailor," he exclaimed, astonished. "How did something that little make a noise that big?"

"She's a mighty mite." Courtney smiled up at him. "Want to feed her?" she offered.

"No! And don't think you can trick me into—into *bonding* with her and with you."

"I wouldn't dream of tricking you into anything. I simply asked if you wanted to feed the baby."

"Aha, so you've switched tactics! Now you're using the candid approach. You think being honest and upfront will disguise your intention to trap me into becoming a *nice little family*," he said, imitating Mrs. Mason's drawl perfectly. "You're trying every approach in the book to induce me to let down my guard, but your motive remains the same—to lure me into that cage marked marriage-and-family."

He thought of the parents who'd raised him, Nina and Dennis McKay, whose detached, distant relationship with its underlying veil of hostility had defined marriage for him. He figured that the McKays must have started out in love at one point to have made it as far as the altar. They'd taken him in as an infant and gone on to have two daughters of their own, but it hadn't worked and the whole family knew it. Dennis McKay had made frequent bitter jokes about marital entrapment; Nina McKay hadn't verbalized her unhappiness, but it had been painfully obvious to all.

Connor had observed and made his own pledge not to delude himself into a situation he couldn't get out of. He'd never come close to it…until now.

"No," he reiterated more forcefully. "It won't happen to me. I won't let it."

"And you said *I'd* flipped? You're the one hatching stupid delusional plots, not me. Save your energy, Connor," Courtney said coolly. "I'm not trying to lure anyone into any metaphorical cage. And I certainly don't want a man who doesn't want me."

Which was true enough in theory, Courtney admitted glumly, but didn't seem to be holding up too well in real life. She remembered those torrid moments in Connor's arms, the way they'd lain together on this very bed…. A sharp, sensual ache ripped through her.

Reflexively she lifted her head and found Connor watching her. Their gazes collided. She had a sinking feeling that her feelings were very much evident in her eyes.

"Anyway, what about Harcourt?" snapped Connor, tearing his eyes away from hers. He'd read the message in them and it took all of his considerable willpower to keep from going to her and taking her into his arms….

But he didn't. He had some principles, after all, and he would not take another man's woman the way his perfidious birth mother had latched onto another woman's husband. He'd come close to doing exactly that earlier today, and he knew it wasn't fair, it wasn't right.

He gave his head a shake, clinging to that belief. He would *not* fall under her spell. But he couldn't help asking, "How is Harcourt going to react to your instant motherhood?"

"He'll undoubtedly wish me well," Courtney replied at once. "Because Emery and I are friends, that's all we've ever been. You've cooked up an imaginary affair between us in your mind, but that's all it's ever been, imaginary and in your mind."

Connor gulped. So she was free. Available. Eminently eligible. She turned him on faster and harder than any woman he'd ever known, and she wanted him. Nobody would be hurt if they got together. There was no reason why they couldn't—except for his own stubborn pledge to remain free and unencumbered from the ties that bind. For a split second he imagined himself taking that chance with Courtney.

But he couldn't, he didn't dare.

At war with himself, Connor turned and walked out the door. He'd used driving as an escape since the day he had received his license, and he resorted to it now. Connor climbed into his car and gunned the engine. He put in the master tape, a cassette tape he'd made of all his favorite songs, and turned up the volume. It was a great tape, and he felt a momentary pang of guilt for not producing it for Courtney when she'd asked for some music. But the songs on this tape reflected too much of him and the way he felt; an insightful person could learn way too much about him from listening. Courtney already knew too much about him.

He stepped on the accelerator and peeled away from the curb.

He replayed his conversation with Wilson Nollier in his mind, over and over again, despite his best attempts to shut it out. A mixture of shame and anger coursed through him, so mixed together that he couldn't begin to separate them. *He'd been glad to hear his position as Richard Tremaine's son validated!* Glad, after all these years of professing to loathe Tremaine. Did that mean he harbored some foolishly sentimental, hopeful and hopeless notion about being reunited with his real father some day? Connor blanched at the very notion.

And if that wasn't difficult enough to deal with, Wilson Nollier, the man he'd reviled as a corrupt baby-seller, had turned out to have a decent, compassionate side, wanting to help an old friend's son, even at his own financial expense. It was almost unbelievable and thoroughly disconcerting, something akin to hearing that Satan didn't mind performing an occasional good deed, just for the hell of it.

Nollier's own good deed had complicated things immensely, though. Courtney had fallen in love with the baby and planned to adopt her! And while part of him scorned her impulsive idealism, Connor admitted that another part admired her generosity and her loving, can-do spirit.

She wasn't the one driving around town, brooding and ambivalent, he noted wryly. She'd made the decision to keep the baby; she was taking care of her; and that was that. Courtney possessed the inner confidence to pull it off, that same inner confidence that

enabled her to handle his temper, to keep his tendency
to dominate from squashing her individuality. The
flash of insight surprised him. He hadn't known her
long, but he felt like he knew her well.

She was a genuinely good person who deserved
someone far better than himself, Connor acknowledged grimly. He was doing her a favor by keeping
his distance. He'd always been uncomfortable around
good girls; he felt he'd corrupt them if he were ever
to become involved with them. He should stick with
his own kind, what he deserved. He certainly didn't
want sweet, loving Courtney's corruption on his conscience.

But he wanted her. Oh, how he wanted her! His
mind filled with pictures of her lying beneath him on
the bed, her body warm and responsive, her mouth
hungry for his, her breasts soft and arching into his
hands, the small nipples pebble-hard. It was all he
could do not to turn the car around and go back to
her. They could put the baby in the crib and pick up
where they'd left off, before Nollier's and Sarah's arrival.

Sarah! Good Lord, now he was even beginning to
think of the baby as Sarah, Courtney's name for her.
If he wasn't careful, she would bamboozle him into
going along with the two-week stay here, and he'd end
up leaving Shadyside Falls a father, a legal adoptive
one. And what could be more natural in this crazy
scheme of things than to marry the baby's adoptive
mother?

He heard the slam of those imaginary cage doors
closing. What a *nice little family* they'd be. He waited
to be repelled and outraged by the very thought of
such a fate. To his great consternation, he felt neither.

Never had he been so restless, so agitated and confused.

With no particular destination in mind, he drove through the town, stopping at the red light at a four-way intersection. The music on the tape, each note, each word, so familiar, began to work its magic and soothe him. This was the way to do it, he assured himself, put everything out of his mind and concentrate on listening to his favorite songs.

The light changed to green, and he pulled into the intersection at the same moment that a sturdy '67 brown sedan, built like a tank, charged through the red light at an astonishing rate of speed.

"Hey!" yelped Connor. He couldn't believe what he was seeing. One trusted traffic to stop at a red light; drivers put their faith in the belief that it was safe to cross the street on green. But the big brown car didn't follow the rules.

Time seemed to slow to a crawl as Connor watched the other car head directly for him. Turning out of its way was futile; pedestrians filled the crosswalks. They were scrambling and screaming at the sight of the renegade car; only if Connor plowed into them could he save himself from being hit. He didn't do it. The noise of the panicky shouts mingled with the sounds of the instruments on the tape. Music to crash by, he thought wryly, resignedly, as the other car smashed into him.

"He's opening his eyes."

"Thank God. Connor, Connor, are you all right?"

"Connor, you gave us all quite a scare, my boy."

"Connor, say something, please! Why isn't he saying anything, Doctor? He's looking right at us, but—"

Connor blinked his eyes and attempted to focus in

the direction of the voices. It hurt to listen, it hurt to blink, it hurt to focus, and the urge to close his eyes and shut out all stimuli was overpowering. He wanted to drift in the thick, slumberous mists enveloping him.

"Mrs. McKay, keep talking to him," said a doctor whose name pin read Dr. T. Standish. He was standing alongside the bed beside an older man and a young woman. "Stimulus is extremely important to keep him from lapsing into a coma."

"A coma?" Courtney's voice broke. She fought back tears.

"There is no reason to frighten Mrs. McKay," Wilson Nollier scolded the doctor. "The X rays showed no brain damage. I have a gut feeling that his diagnosis is just what the ER doctor said—a concussion and nothing more."

"We'll know more after the MRI," countered Dr. Standish. He turned to Courtney. "MRI is short for Magnetic Resonance Imagery. It's a state-of-the-art diagnostic tool and can detect a subtle injury to the brain that might have eluded the less definitive X rays. Mr. McKay is the next on the schedule."

"Those machines don't come cheap," added Nollier, glaring at the doctor. "Perhaps you should keep in mind that a small community hospital like Shadyside Falls would never own one if my firm hadn't donated three-fourths of the cost for it."

"I'm well aware that you're one of the hospital's most generous benefactors, Mr. Nollier," the doctor said tautly.

Courtney was tired of their squabbling. Ignoring them both, she leaned over Connor's bed, took his hand in hers and squeezed. "Connor, please, wake up! Open your eyes and look at me. Please!"

Slowly Connor opened his eyes again, responding to the urgency in her voice, to the warm pressure of her hand in his. She was very close to him, and he could see the tears in her huge dark eyes. Gypsy eyes, he thought, and wondered who she was. At that particular moment, he didn't know who he was, either. But he was too groggy to worry about it.

"Oh, Connor!" Courtney cried, relief flowing through her as she gazed into his beautiful sea-green eyes. "Do you remember the accident?"

"No," he admitted dazedly. "Is that why I'm here? An accident?"

"A car accident," she confirmed. "As soon as you were brought into the hospital, Dr. Martin—he's on the staff here, the one who delivered Sarah—recognized your name and notified Wilson Nollier on his car phone. He was on his way to Washington, but he turned around and picked me up at Mrs. Mason's place and we came straight here. You've been unconscious about an hour and—"

"My head!" Connor interrupted with a groan. The mists were receding, but a powerful throbbing pain in his head erupted with volcanic force.

"I bet you have the granddaddy of all headaches, Connor, my boy," Wilson Nollier said sympathetically. "Your head was banged against the window when that old man hit you. The police said if you hadn't been wearing your seat belt you would have been seriously hurt."

Connor groaned. "As opposed to what?" His head hurt so badly he wanted to scream with pain, but he had neither the strength nor the energy to do so.

"Oh, Connor!" He sounded so like his old self—weaker, of course, but still droll—that Courtney began to cry, letting the tears she'd been rigidly holding at bay slide down her cheeks. "I've been so worried about you."

"Connor," he repeated dreamily. "Me?"

Courtney glanced in horror at Wilson Nollier. The attorney inhaled sharply.

"Now, what's this? Of course, your name is Connor. Connor McKay," Nollier said with a hearty laugh that sounded both forced and false. "Are you having a bit of fun with us, son?"

The doctor pulled up his eyelids, one by one, and shone a pencil-thin light into each eye. "Mr. McKay, do you know where you are?"

Another stunning jolt of pain made him wince. "In a hospital, obviously," he rasped.

"You're in Shadyside Falls Hospital," the doctor supplied helpfully. "You were in a car accident—"

"Poor old Herman Meredith got hold of the keys to his wife's car," added Nollier. "He's eighty-nine years old, has Alzheimer's disease and hasn't driven for the past ten years. No one knows what possessed him to get into that car today, but he ended up running a red light and hitting you broadside."

"There were dozens of eyewitnesses," Courtney added tearfully. "They all said how brave you were not to turn your car out of his path. You would've hit a group of pedestrians, including a number of small children. Instead, you let him hit you and saved those people!"

So he was a hero, of sorts? Connor contemplated that for a moment. But he still didn't remember any of it.

"Do you know who the president of the United States is?" Dr. Standish pressed.

Connor told him the president's name.

"And who was president before that?" the doctor asked.

"Who cares?" snapped Nollier. "Ask him something relevant. Like who is Richard Tremaine?"

Connor thought about it. "I don't know." He saw the anxiety and fear in both the young woman's and the older man's faces. "Should I know?" he asked.

Nobody answered him.

"Mr. McKay, Connor, do you know who she is?" Dr. Standish interjected, pointing to the pretty, dark-haired young woman who was still clutching his hand.

Connor stared at her, though the effort of doing so made his head ache more. She was a knockout, he decided, though the term made his temples throb in protest. "No," he said softly.

Right now she looked scared to death, and he wanted to comfort her. And though he seemed to possess no personal knowledge of himself, he instinctively knew she was the kind of woman he could fall in love with.

"Connor, she's your wife!" Wilson Nollier exclaimed. He appeared genuinely distraught. "Your wife Courtney. You've been married for five years, you both wanted a child, and finally, today, you were blessed with a beautiful baby daughter. I believe you're naming her—Sarah?" He glanced at Courtney for confirmation and she nodded. "Connor, try to remember!" he urged.

Connor tried but nothing came. Though he felt that strong connection and attraction to her, he couldn't actually remember her as his wife. There were no memories at all, not of the accident or of a wife named Courtney or a baby daughter named Sarah. The fog blanketing his brain began to lift, and the seriousness of the situation struck him with full force. *He didn't know who he was!*

"I can't remember anything," he said, panic creeping into his voice. He looked at the woman called Courtney. "You had a baby today?" Though his memory seemed to have been erased, somehow he knew that she looked amazingly fit for a woman who had just experienced childbirth.

"No," Courtney said quickly.

"You're adopting the baby," Wilson Nollier added. He hit his forehead with the palm of his hand. "Damn, this is terrible! A tragedy!"

Agitated now, Connor tried to sit up, but the severe pain in his head made him fall back on the pillows. A wave of nausea rolled over him and he began to perspire.

"Mr. Nollier, if you can't control your outbursts, I'm going to have to ask you to leave the room," Dr. Standish said sternly. "You're upsetting the patient."

"Hell, he'd be brain-dead if he weren't upset," retorted Nollier. "He has amnesia! I never really believed amnesia existed, I thought it was a stupid plot device used by hack writers. But here's poor Connor who doesn't know who he is or who his wife is. He doesn't know—"

"Mrs. McKay, tell your husband something about his job," the doctor interjected. "You'd be surprised what small fact might suddenly click and stimulate his memory."

His job? Courtney was aghast. If she said that Connor scrounged up facts for *Insight* magazine and TV tabloid shows like *Inside Copy* and the like, Wilson Nollier might become suspicious of their motives in approaching him about adoption. And if he got suspicious, he might become defensive and feel threatened and find a way to neutralize the threat. *The threat being her and Connor.*

With Connor, an amnesiac in the hospital, and herself staying with Mrs. Mason, Nollier's henchman—henchperson?—they would be pitifully easy targets. And they had baby Sarah to consider as well. Perhaps she'd seen one too many couple-in-jeopardy movies, which was making her wrongfully paranoid, but Courtney decided that she didn't dare risk the truth.

She remembered Connor teasing her on the drive to Shadyside Falls earlier. *"What if I were to tell you that I worked my way through college and law school? That I passed the bar exam and am a licensed attorney in Virginia, Maryland and the District of Columbia?"*

It wasn't true, of course, but couldn't she use it to divert Nollier? "He—he's a lawyer," she said quickly, mentally asking Connor's forgiveness for deceiving him along with Nollier.

"I didn't realize Connor was a lawyer," said Nollier. "We didn't get into occupations and professions during your office visit."

"No, we didn't," said Courtney. Vital issues such as employment, family background and references had not been mentioned at all. She and Connor had been appalled, for it had confirmed their belief that Wilson Nollier was only interested in the cash he would receive from the prospective adoptive parents.

That meeting seemed a thousand years ago, when Nollier had been their enemy. Now, strangely enough, in the time since Connor's accident, she'd begun to view the attorney as an ally. He certainly seemed genuinely concerned and upset about Connor's plight.

Still, her every instinct warned her to keep the truth about themselves a secret. Wilson Nollier was a powerful man with contacts everywhere, particularly, it seemed, in this town. For Connor's safety, for little Sarah's sake, she had to let him go on believing that she and Connor really were married. No, Nollier must not find out their true motives for coming to Shadyside Falls.

"Does Connor work for a law firm or the government?" Nollier asked. "Does he have his own practice?"

Courtney bit her lip. She knew next to nothing about law, and if she goofed, Wilson Nollier could really nail her. "Sometimes he—uh—represents clients like—like National Public Broadcasting," she said slowly, trying to remember something, anything, about lawyers from episodes of TV shows she'd seen.

"So he sometimes deals with the entertainment industry?" Nollier seized on that. "Does he have any celebrity clients? What case was a particular landmark for him?"

"He—uh—drew up the contract between NPB and Sinead Halleran, the Irish folksinger," Courtney said. At least she was fabricating on a little firmer ground now. She had been a production assistant on the NPB filmed concert featuring Halleran and a marvelous Gaelic flutist. "He was very excited about that," she added, striving for credibility. "We, uh, both were."

Connor looked blank. "I'm sorry, I have no recollection of any of it."

It tore her apart to see him look so sad, so helpless. Courtney fought back another round of tears. Of course he didn't remember, it hadn't happened! But she didn't dare tell him, not with Wilson Nollier standing there.

"Never heard of Sinead Halleran. I don't watch much television, not even NPB," Nollier said apologetically.

Courtney breathed a sigh of relief. Nollier's lack of familiarity with NPB could only work to her advantage, especially since she'd invented an imaginary legal career for Connor there!

A nurse entered the room and motioned the doctor, who followed her out. Courtney and Nollier looked at each other, then at Connor, who had closed his eyes and was lying very still in the bed.

"Courtney, I want you to know that I'm going to do everything I can to help," Nollier said quietly. "I'll make certain that Meredith's insurance company handles the hospital bill, and I insist on picking up your expenses here in Shadyside Falls."

Courtney swallowed hard. "And Sarah? As you know, Mrs. Mason is taking care of her now but—" she paused and took a deep breath "—I don't know how to say this, I hope it doesn't sound overblown and melodramatic, but I love her already. I don't want to lose her."

"My dear, you're not going to. That paperwork will be processed as planned. You and Connor are keeping your baby."

Dr. Standish returned to the room with the nurse and two orderlies. "We're taking him down to the MRI for the brain scan now," he announced.

Connor's head ached; he was nauseated from the movement of being transferred from the bed to the gurney. He felt depressed and alone. Having no memory had plunged him into a dark abyss where nobody or nothing else existed but himself, and it was the most terrible feeling in the world. He glanced bleakly at Courtney, who was watching him through tear-filled eyes.

Their gazes held.

Suddenly Courtney slipped between the orderlies to stand beside the gurney. "Connor, everything is going to be all right," she said fervently, reaching for his hand. She carried it to her lips and pressed her mouth against his palm.

"I love you," she said impulsively. The words tumbled out, unrehearsed and unplanned. Was she so caught up in playing the role of loving wife that she'd ad-libbed what such a character would most surely say at such a moment? she wondered.

Connor managed a slight smile. Her words were a soothing balm, warming him and banishing the deep despair that threatened to engulf him. He wasn't so alone, after all, he consoled himself. He had a wife who loved him, they had a child.

"Will you be here when I get back?" he murmured. He realized at that moment how lucky he was to have someone who loved him, someone who really cared. What if he'd had to face this ordeal alone and unloved, lying here in the hospital with no knowledge of his past or present, and his future a terrifying blank?

"Of course I'll be here," Courtney said. She leaned down and kissed his cheek.

Connor put his hand on her head and stroked her soft, dark hair. "I'm glad." He felt buoyed, reassured and sought to reassure her. "Don't worry, Courtney. Everything really is going to be all right."

Courtney held herself together until he was wheeled out of the room. Then she buried her face in her hands and wept.

Eight

The elevator doors snapped open, and Courtney, carrying Sarah strapped in her bulky car seat, stepped into the hospital corridor. A big plastic shopping bag and a canvas diaper bag dangled from her wrists, hitting her legs as she walked. Connor's room was halfway down the hall, and when she looked up, she saw him walking toward her.

He was wearing the blue pajamas she'd found in his suitcase and brought in for him and the belted navy silk robe that Wilson Nollier had given him. He looked virile and fit, certainly not anybody's idea of a patient. He waved to her, his face wreathed in smiles.

Courtney's breath caught in her throat. When he smiled at her in that particular way, she went all soft and weak inside. He was so handsome, so sexy, so irresistibly appealing. The intensity of her feelings staggered her. She felt light-headed, torn between laughter and tears.

The week since Connor's accident had been the strangest she'd ever spent. She was living a lie, and deception had always repulsed her; she was taking risks, and she had always gone for safety and control. Her life was a complete paradox, yet this past week had been nothing short of—of *wonderful.*

Connor thought she was his wife, and he wanted her with him all the time. His face lit up at the sight of her; he was loving and thoughtful and considerate toward her and the baby. They took advantage of the hospital's liberal visiting hours to spend all day and most of the evening together. Baby Sarah stayed with them the entire time, and they took turns holding and feeding her. Courtney was convinced he enjoyed taking care of the baby as much as she did. He proudly showed her off to the nurses, calling her his daughter.

The cause of his amnesia remained a mystery. After days of extensive testing and observation, the doctors could find no physical reason for it. Although he had suffered a concussion, there had been no discernible damage to his brain. His general memory was fine; he'd retained his social and intellectual skills and could function independently as an adult in the world. His overall health was excellent. Even his headaches had faded.

Since brain damage had been ruled out, Dr. Ammon, the neuropsychiatrist who'd examined him, had another theory. He believed that Connor was experiencing selective amnesia, a disassociative state brought on by the blow to his head, in which unrecognized, unexpressed feelings and needs had temporarily short-circuited an overloaded consciousness.

Courtney and Wilson Nollier had exchanged glances, their eyes glazing as Dr. Ammon continued his lengthy, jargon-filled lecture.

"Cut the psycho-babble and explain it in English," Nollier snapped.

"In a disassociative state, the conscious mind goes blank," the doctor explained, directing his remark to Courtney and ignoring Nollier's exclamation of disdain. "It's involuntary, a temporary psychological escape from an extremely stressful situation. In this case, I believe that finally adopting a child was the trigger. After five years of trying and failing to give his wife a baby, the dream was finally realized, but not through his own sexual potency. I find it extremely significant that upon regaining consciousness and being reminded of the child, Mr. McKay asked his wife if she had given birth."

Courtney and Nollier stared skeptically at the doctor but made no comment.

But Dr. Ammon didn't seem to mind their lack of input. *"Given birth!"* he continued enthusiastically. "Why, it's practically a textbook case. His mind blocked out the infertility problems of the past along with all the pain and failure. In this new reality, he was able to achieve fecundity! And as he has no physical brain damage preventing it, conscious memory will return when the subconscious finally comes to terms with the painful reality."

"What a lot of mumbo jumbo!" Nollier hooted. "How come you headshrinkers are always so hung up on sex?"

It wasn't a bad theory, Courtney thought, except it was completely untrue. She had another guilt attack for allowing the doctors to believe what Nollier had told them about their alleged marriage. Yet the more she pondered the doctor's explanation, she realized that the disassociative state of amnesia theory could fit in another context. Before the accident, Nollier and Connor had talked about Richard Tremaine—stirring up potentially explosive feelings? Now Connor remembered nothing about either of his fathers.

She thought he seemed happier, his cynical and bitter edge had disappeared. Could she possibly be right?

As for Connor, he was eager to leave the hospital. He told the doctors that he was convinced his memory would return when he was living full-time with his wife and child. Every evening when visiting hours were over and he walked Courtney to the elevator, carrying the baby in his arms, he would kiss them both goodbye and say how much he wanted to go with them.

And each night Courtney lay alone in her bed in Mrs. Mason's house, tossing and turning restlessly, worrying about what would happen when his memory returned. With Wilson Nollier a daily visitor—the attorney continued to faithfully make the drive from D.C.—she didn't dare reveal the truth to Connor.

Last night, staring out the window during those long, lonely hours, Courtney forced herself to face the shameful truth. She didn't want to tell Connor the truth and end their "marriage." The threat of Nollier had become less a danger and more of an excuse she was using to prolong the fantasy.

And if Connor's memory never returned? She tried to stifle the spark of hope she felt at that prospect. It was wrong, she scolded herself, it was selfish and unfair. Connor deserved the right to decide his own fate and live his own life. But when his memory returned, she knew he would leave her and Sarah and go off on his own, back to his stupid job and his affairs with no strings. And there was no way she could stifle the sadness she felt at that prospect.

"You've been shopping this morning, I see." Connor greeted her in the hall with a smile and a quick kiss on the cheek. He took the baby and the cumbersome car seat from her, leaning down to brush his lips across Sarah's small forehead.

Courtney delved into the bags as they walked into his room. "There's a cute children's clothing shop in town. I bought a few things for Sarah." She pulled out a dainty flowered sunsuit and matching bonnet, a yellow pinafore with duck appliqués and an adorable lavender dress she'd been unable to resist. "I bought them all two sizes larger than what she's wearing now so they'll fit her this summer."

This summer. Courtney's heart turned over. Would Connor be around this summer to see Sarah wear them? Probably not. She swallowed back the lump that sprang to her throat.

Connor unwrapped the baby from the blankets and quilted snowsuit, which Courtney had bundled her in. "Don't you think she's a bit overdressed? She could survive an Arctic blizzard in this gear," he remarked dryly. "It's April, Courtney, not January. One thing I know is the correct date. The doctors and nurses mention it every time they come into the room to *orient* me to time."

The carefully recited dates had become a private joke with them. Courtney smiled. "I know it's *April 13*, but there was a chill in the air this morning when I left the house. I didn't want Sarah to catch cold."

Connor hoisted Sarah into his arms, smiling into the

baby's blue-eyed gaze. "You feel ten pounds lighter now, don't you, Cookie?"

The baby made a gurgling noise and Connor laughed. "She says, 'Thanks, Dad.'"

Courtney smiled. She loved watching Connor play with Sarah. He'd nicknamed her Cookie because he claimed she was sweet and soft like one. He had a propensity for nicknames, she thought, remembering how he'd called her Gypsy almost from the moment they'd met. Though she had claimed it annoyed her, she realized that she missed hearing it.

"You look sad." Holding the baby in the crook of one arm, Connor slipped his other hand around the nape of Courtney's neck. "What's the matter, Courtney?"

She was going to have to be more careful, more on guard, Courtney admonished herself. When they were together, Connor watched her intently, seldom taking his eyes off her. He was quick to pick up the tiniest nuance in her facial expressions and inflections of her voice.

He began to massage her nape. "I know how hard this has been on you, sweetheart. Spending all day and all evening here at the hospital with me and then getting up at night with the baby."

"I don't mind, Connor," she protested. "I'm fine, really."

But she wasn't fine; she felt dangerously overemotional. And his caressing fingers were causing ripples of fire to spread from her belly to her breasts and then shoot lower, deeper. She knew she should move away from him, but she couldn't bring herself to do it. What he was doing felt entirely too good.

"You're very brave and very strong, Courtney,"

Connor said huskily. "I don't know how I could've gotten through this past week without you. But it's time to let me take over, to let me take care of you and the baby. Time to let me be a husband and father instead of a patient."

"Oh, Connor," she whispered. If only it could be true! With a small, shuddery moan, she let her head rest against his strong, broad shoulder, giving into the fantasy, if only for a little while.

He slid his hand down the length of her spine, kneaded the curve of her waist for several long, sensuous moments, then spread his hand flat across her belly. She was wearing a cherry-red rayon skirt, and the warm imprint of his palm permeated the soft material. A sharp, searing pleasure licked through her.

"I think about you all the time," he said softly, his mouth feathering her temple, her hair, with soft, light kisses. "I want you—to hold you and kiss you and touch you. Lying in bed here alone at night—" He laughed deeply, his voice warm and sexy, and added, "There's one part of me that doesn't seem to be having any trouble...remembering."

He suggestively pressed her against him and she gasped, feeling deliciously sandwiched between the warm pressure of his hand on her abdomen and his virile hardness behind her. Automatically she laid her hand over his.

"I'm aching for you, gypsy eyes," he groaned, taking her earlobe between his teeth in a teasing, sensual bite.

She felt dizzy, disoriented, as if she'd just staggered off the Tilt-a-Whirl at the amusement park. "W-What?"

"You have the biggest, darkest, most beautiful

eyes," he said softly, mesmerizingly, slowly moving his hand higher, gliding closer, closer to her breasts. He stopped, resting his hand just below them.

"It's weird, isn't it?" he said wryly. "That I know gypsies have dark eyes but I have no knowledge of my own parents. That I know the president's name but had to be told my own."

"The doctors said—"

"I don't want to talk about the doctors. I'm tired of doctors and I'm tired of this hospital. I want to get out of this place today. I want my life back." His hand moved those crucial inches and closed over her breast. "I want my wife back."

Her gaze dropped to see his big hand cupping her through the cherry-red rayon blouse, and the sight was as stimulating as the feel of his fingers fondling her. With unerring accuracy, his thumb found her nipple and began to rub sensually, bringing it to a throbbing peak. Courtney squirmed against him and a whimper escaped from her lips.

Sarah chose that moment to remind them of her presence, opening her small mouth and letting out a distinct wail. Reluctantly Connor dropped his hand. "It seems we have a little chaperone," he said, turning his full attention to the infant. "Hmm, a damp one."

"I'll change her," Courtney said quickly, stumbling away from him to pick up the canvas diaper bag filled with baby supplies. Her hands were trembling; her knees, too.

"Let's take her for a walk in the hall," she suggested after the baby was diapered and dry again. She felt too nervous and high-strung to be alone with Connor. Her whole body was aflame with longing, and her instantaneous response to him left her feeling exposed and vulnerable.

Things were complicated enough, she lectured herself. Adding sex to this mess was as risky—and as crazy!—as tossing a match into a pool of gasoline. She needed people around. There was safety—and self-control—in a crowd.

"Sarah wants to show the nurses her new clothes," Courtney said in a high, strained voice quite unlike her normal tone. "We—"

"Sarah is ready for a nap," Connor interrupted. He laid the baby on her tummy in the portable white wicker bassinet that they kept in the corner of the room for her. Wilson Nollier had brought it in the first night of Connor's hospitalization.

"She's not sleepy." Courtney went to pick her up. But Sarah was not going to come to her rescue this time. Her big blue eyes had already closed.

Courtney straightened and turned around. Connor was standing directly behind her, so close that they were almost touching. "She's asleep." Her voice shook. "I—I guess our shopping trip this morning wore her out."

"So it seems." Connor smiled lazily, his voice deep and low. "And now, picking up where we left off..." He slid one arm around her waist and drew her slowly to him.

Their eyes met and held for a long, sexually charged moment. A wealth of wordless communication passed between them.

Courtney went to him. She knew she shouldn't, she could recite a whole list of reasons why not. But reason, along with caution and resolve, dissolved when he was looking at her in *that* particular way. Desire shone bright and hot in his eyes, and his wide, sexy mouth was curved into a smile that made her breathless.

No man had ever had such power over her, and it was more than a little scary. But it was wildly exciting, as well. He pulled her close, and through the thin fabric of her skirt, she could feel the muscular hardness of his thighs pressing against her.

"Courtney." His warm breath stirred her hair as he lowered his head and brushed his lips across her forehead.

Her eyes dropped closed, and she felt his featherlight kisses on her lids, on her cheeks, along the fine line of her jaw. As if in a dream, she slid her arms slowly around his neck. She stroked his neck with her fingers, running them through the sandy-brown thickness of his hair. It felt so good to hold him, to be in his arms.

And then his mouth took hers, warm and hard and commanding. Her lips parted on impact and his tongue penetrated the moist softness of her mouth, rubbing against her tongue in a seductive, suggestive rhythm.

Passion surged through her and she clung to him, holding him tighter, and moving wantonly against him. Her nipples were taut and sensitive and strained against the material of her clothes. She felt a shocking urge to bare her breasts and feel his hands on her, his mouth....

Trembling with urgency, she smoothed her hands over his back, savoring the hard male feel of him. It was intoxicating to touch him like this, to know that he wanted her. As she wanted him.

Connor drew a deep, shuddering breath and deepened the kiss, pulling her blouse from the waistband of her skirt to slip his hand under it. He cupped her breast, possessively, ardently, and caressed the tight bud of her nipple. When he thrust his thigh between hers and applied a firm, seductive pressure, she whimpered at the exquisite pleasure of it.

"You're so sweet," Connor said huskily, nibbling on her neck as his hands molded her ever-closer to his hard masculine frame. "So sexy and passionate. And you're mine!" he added possessively. "My darling, my wife."

She wanted to melt into him, she wanted to lie down on the bed with him and make love. But his words set off alarm bells in her head. She was getting too caught up in their role-playing; the edge between fantasy and reality was becoming dangerously blurred. She wanted his words to be as true as his passion.

And they weren't, they couldn't be. She was most certainly not his wife. The real Connor McKay didn't want a wife; he was allergic to commitment. And when his memory returned and he was faced with these days of himself as a loving, caring husband and father, he would not call her his darling. He would probably try to sue her for fraud!

Nervously Courtney pulled herself out of his arms. She turned her back to him as she readjusted her clothes with trembling hands. "Connor, I—we—"

"It's all right, sweetheart." He cupped her shoulders with his big hands and dropped a lingering kiss on the nape of her neck. "I know this isn't the time or place. I got a little carried away." He folded his arms around her waist and pulled her back against him, holding her tight. "You have that effect on me, Courtney. All my instincts tell me that you always have. And always will, my love."

His words, so loving and sexy, warmed her and made her sigh. She permitted herself the luxury of remaining in his arms for a few more blissful moments before reluctantly moving away from him.

"I bought something else while I was in town," she said with a little too much forced gaiety. She was desperate to refocus her thoughts on something other than how much she wanted to be in his arms.

She pulled a game of checkers from the bag. "Since you turned out to be such a card shark and can beat me at every game, I thought we'd try something else, something *I* can win. It's only fair to warn you that I was a notorious checkers-shark when I was a kid."

The occupational therapist had given Connor a deck of cards. He'd retained complete memory—and playing skills—of countless card games that he couldn't remember learning. He and Courtney often played cards during their visits, and he won each game soundly.

"And you're hoping to take advantage of a poor amnesiac to secure a win?" Connor challenged, sounding so much like his old self that Courtney started. "I don't think so, honey. Let the competition begin."

They played two games—he won one and she won the other—and were in the middle of the tiebreaker when a team of doctors and nurses swept into the room. Wilson Nollier was leading the pack.

Courtney tensed. She was always on edge when Nollier was present, though Connor accepted him easily, believing him to be the "friend" the attorney claimed he was. Nollier was forever asking questions about Connor's past—about his childhood, his job, their marriage—in order to "jog" Connor's memory.

She answered them to the best of her ability, trying to cover her lapses—of which there were so many, as she didn't have a great deal of information about Connor's life prior to his meeting her.

And of course, anything she said about their marriage was pure fiction. She hated to lie and feared getting caught in the web she'd had to spin. Odd, but during the long hours she spent alone with Connor, there was no tension and no need to lie. He didn't ask her any questions about himself or their past. It was as if his life had begun afresh in the hospital room and he had no interest in what had happened before.

Connor was interested in hearing about her, though, and Courtney told him about her family and growing up all over the world, about her job at NPB, even about Mark and Marianne's desperate quest for a baby. He listened intently and remembered everything she told him, often discussing it with her later.

But now, here was Wilson Nollier with the medical team to intrude on their privacy once more. Courtney barely managed to suppress a disgruntled sigh.

Wilson Nollier didn't notice her less-than-enthusiastic welcome; he never did. "Great news!" he exclaimed with even more ebullience than usual. "You're going home today, Connor!"

"Yes, Connor. Today's the day," seconded Dr. Standish. "April 13. You're being discharged this afternoon."

"Of course, you'll stay here in Shadyside Falls another week, as originally planned, while Sarah's paperwork is being processed," Nollier chimed in. "Anyway, Standish here would like to see you several times before he turns your case over to a physician in D.C."

"I can leave the hospital now?" Connor repeated. He caught Courtney's hand and drew her to his side. "That's the best news I've heard since—hmm, it's hard to come up with an effective comparison when I only have a one-week memory span to draw upon."

Nollier laughed delightedly. "You've kept your sense of humor throughout. You've been a true champion, Connor. I'm proud of you. Your father is, too. I've kept him informed daily of your progress, of course. He'd like to visit you. Is that all right with you, Connor?"

Connor shrugged. "Sure, why not?"

"He wanted to come as soon as I told him about the accident, but I knew you'd want to be out of the hospital before meeting—er, *seeing*—him," continued Wilson. "He'll come to Mrs. Mason's place tomorrow morning at ten, if that suits you."

Connor nodded. "It's all right with me."

"I don't think it's a good idea," Courtney interjected, shooting Nollier a glare. She was angry on Connor's behalf. It wasn't fair for him to meet Richard Tremaine while in such a vulnerable state. If his memory was intact, he would never agree to it and Nollier knew it!

She felt the eyes of everybody in the room upon her, including Connor's. Uh-oh. Now she had to come up with a reasonable explanation as to why her husband shouldn't visit with his father.

"We haven't mentioned this before, but there has been some—uh—*tension* between Connor and his father in the past." That was true, in an understated sort of way, wasn't it? Lord, how she hated to lie! "I think we should postpone this visit until Connor is... stronger."

"I'm strong already, Courtney. You mean until I get my memory back," Connor corrected her. "Sweetheart, it's okay. I've already figured out that something wasn't quite right between my family and me. I've seen the way you tense up when Wilson asks you about them. I've deliberately refrained from asking you anything about them, and I've noticed that you haven't volunteered anything, either, trying to spare me any anxiety, I'm sure."

"Oh, Connor." Courtney groaned. He'd misinterpreted everything!

"I appreciate your trying to protect me, darling." He hugged her to him. "But it's not necessary. I want to see my father. Since I have no memory of what's happened before, I'd like to take the opportunity to make a new start."

He wouldn't be saying that if knew the whole truth, Courtney knew. Her heart began to pound. "Connor, I think you should know that the problem between you and your father is a little more serious than something like your dad attending a business meeting instead of your sixth birthday party, or being on the road instead of catching your school play. You two—"

"What Connor said about a new start makes excellent sense," Nollier cut in. "He's a rational, functioning adult, Courtney. He can make his own decisions and he has."

"How functioning can he be when he can't remember anything but the past week?" Courtney challenged.

"You're very protective of your husband, and that's good," Nollier said soothingly. "I'm happy that Connor has a wife who so fiercely cares about him. But this time you're being *over*protective, Courtney.

Richard is desperate to see his son, and Connor has agreed to see him. It's going to happen.''

"Connor didn't agree, he was railroaded into it,'' she retorted. "And I—''

"I almost forgot,'' Nollier said, cutting her off. "I have news for you, too, Courtney.'' A wide grin curved his mouth. "Wonderful news. Remember when you and Connor were talking about your brother and his wife and how much they want to adopt a baby? Well, I kept it in mind because you two young people have come to mean a lot to me and I want to help both you and your respective families. So call your brother and tell him that he'll be a father within the month. There is a young girl who came to my office looking for a prospective adoptive family....''

"Still mad at Wilson?'' Connor asked.

The expression on Courtney's face gave him his answer before she vehemently replied, "Yes!''

"It was an incredibly obvious bribery attempt on Wilson's part.'' Connor grinned, remembering. "He didn't say it, but the implied message was definitely, 'Your brother will have the child he and his wife have been longing for *if* you'll stop making a fuss about Connor's father visiting.'''

"It was unconscionable!'' Courtney exclaimed.

They were having dinner at Tell's Inn, Shadyside Falls's most popular restaurant, celebrating Connor's first meal since his release from the hospital. Mrs. Mason had insisted on baby-sitting Sarah while they dined.

Connor reached across the table and placed his hand over hers. "Sweetheart, stop worrying. I promise I won't become unglued when my father arrives tomorrow." He smiled wryly. "How can I? I have no memory of him."

Truer words had never been spoken, Courtney thought grimly. And amnesia had nothing to do with Connor's lack of memories with his father. Ever since Wilson Nollier had announced Richard Tremaine's impending visit, she had been debating whether or not to tell Connor part of the truth—that he'd never met the man who had fathered him, that he'd been raised by another man. But Dr. Ammon's description of disassociative amnesia stopped her.

Suppose Connor subconsciously wanted to know and acknowledge Richard Tremaine as his father; the blow to his head and subsequent amnesia gave him the ideal chance to do so, without the bitterness of the past blocking the way.

"When the subconscious finally comes to terms with the painful reality, conscious memory will return," Dr. Ammon had said. Would meeting Richard Tremaine and establishing some sort of rapport with him enable Connor to do that? He really seemed to want to see his father. Would she be doing more harm than good by interfering in any way? Or was that a self-deluding, self-serving theory, designed to ease her conscience as she continued the charade between them?

"It's just so complicated!" she said, more to herself than to him. "I want to do the right thing...."

Her voice trailed off. Here she sat, having dinner at a cozy table for two and holding hands with him, playing the part of his wife, duping him into playing the part of her husband—and she had the nerve to even *talk* about doing the right thing? She looked at him, her dark eyes troubled. "Connor, I don't know what to do. I've always been forthright and honest. I've never—''

''I want you to stop worrying,'' Connor interrupted. He lifted her hand to his lips and kissed her fingertips. ''Everything you're doing is what you should be doing, what you have to do. Stop tormenting yourself, baby.''

She desperately wanted to believe him. But of course, she couldn't. ''You don't know the half of it,'' she said ruefully. ''There are circumstances—''

''This is supposed to be a celebration. We're not going to talk about anything more serious than what's on the menu tonight,'' Connor cut in again. ''And how glad I am to be sprung from the hospital.''

''But, Connor, I—''

He squeezed her hand. ''Promise that you won't address me in the first person plural, as in 'How are *we* feeling today?' and 'Did *we* enjoy our meal?' Hospital patient-speak is a hellacious language,'' he added dryly.

''Connor, I'm afraid that you—''

''They have fresh Virginia spots on the menu. What a welcome change from the hospital's rubber chicken. Have you thought about an appetizer?''

She stared into his eyes. ''You're determined to keep me from—''

''Wailing and wringing your hands over a situation that's beyond your control.'' His gaze held hers. ''Yes, Courtney, I'm determined to do that.''

And he did, successfully blocking every attempt she made to discuss their situation and his condition. Finally she gave up and gave into his wishes. They talked about the menu, about Sarah, about the news they'd watched on television, about his prowess at cards and hers at checkers, for she'd won that crucial third game. Connor demanded a rematch, then drew a ticktacktoe board on the back of the paper place mat and challenged her to a match.

When they finished dinner, he suggested a walk through town before heading back to Mrs. Mason's house in the rental car that Wilson Nollier had procured for Courtney immediately following the accident. Holding hands, they strolled along the main street of Shadyside Falls, pausing to window-shop as they went. Connor was charming, funny and attentive, and Courtney couldn't help responding to him.

It was as if he were courting her and she was very willing to be courted. As they walked together, talking and laughing and holding hands, Courtney gazed up at him and finally admitted the truth to herself: she was deeply in love with Connor McKay.

Nine

"The little one wasn't a bit of trouble," Mrs. Mason assured them when they arrived back at the house an hour later. "She finished her bottle about forty minutes ago and went straight to sleep. Did you two enjoy your evening out?"

Connor smiled warmly at Courtney. "We had a great time." He pulled a ten-dollar bill from his wallet and handed it to Mrs. Mason. "I hope we didn't keep you up too late."

"Not at all." Mrs. Mason tucked the money into the pocket of her housedress. "I'm going to turn in now, but if you'd like to stay downstairs and use the kitchen or the living room, feel free."

"Thanks, but we'll call it a night, too." Connor caught Courtney's hand and headed toward the stairway.

Courtney's heart jumped into her throat. Her knees

were suddenly so weak and shaky it was hard to walk, let alone keep up with Connor's swift pace.

Connor thought he was her husband, he believed they had a normal marriage, a good marriage. He had every intention of sharing the queen-sized bed in their room, and she could come up with no credible reason to tell him why he couldn't.

The medical excuse she might have used had been demolished when Connor had left the hospital this afternoon. "There is no reason why you can't resume sexual relations as soon as you want," Dr. Standish had said matter-of-factly, while Courtney's pulse had gone into overdrive. Now the doctor's words replayed through her head.

No reason? They weren't married, was that reason enough? *Resume?* She was a virgin who had never experienced sexual relations in the first place. *As soon as you want?* Connor made it plain that he wanted, all right.

But she wanted him just as badly, Courtney acknowledged as frissons of heat rippled through her. The sexual excitement or infatuation or whatever her initial feelings for him could be called had swiftly and irrevocably deepened. She was in love with him.

Thus, another complication was added to this already impossibly complicated situation. How did a woman keep the man she loved, the man whose touch she yearned for, out of her bed?

Did she even want to?

"Let's check on the baby," Connor suggested, leading her into the small room adjoining theirs. Sarah was sleeping peacefully on her stomach, her tiny arms resting above her head.

"She's so beautiful, so precious," Courtney whispered, standing beside the crib and gazing down at her. "She looks like a little angel, doesn't she?"

"Our baby," Connor murmured, his voice filled with awe. He and Courtney were going to raise this child together. They would watch her grow from a helpless infant to a child to a young woman. She would learn to walk and to talk, to laugh and to love, to become a mature, compassionate adult who would someday have a family of her own, continuing the process that he and Courtney were beginning right now.

He felt immensely privileged to be a part of this transmission of life and love. A wave of sheer happiness surged through him, and he linked his arms around Courtney's waist, resting his hands on the flat plain of her stomach. "I'm the luckiest man in the world," he said huskily, nuzzling her neck.

Courtney intertwined her fingers with his and leaned into him, her heart overflowing with love for him. Her eyes filled with tears. "Oh, Connor, if only—"

"None of that," he interrupted softly. "We have each other and our beautiful baby. I don't need my memory back to know how fortunate we are."

Courtney released a shuddering sob and he tightened his hold on her. And then it happened. A flashback.

He'd had some in the hospital that he had mentioned to the doctors but had purposely kept from Courtney. There was no use raising her hopes, and oddly enough, the flashbacks had nothing to do with her; they were snippets from his childhood, from his college and law school years. He actually remembered his graduation from the University of Maryland Law School and his elation when he'd learned that he had passed the bar. There were no memories of how he had used his law degree or of his professional life, but the doctors had assured him all of that would return in time.

In the flash of memory he was experiencing now, he saw himself driving, he even heard which song was playing on the tape. His heart leapt. Was he going to remember the accident? He had listened to it described so often that he found himself anticipating the big brown car speeding through the red light.

But the only thing filling his mind was memories of himself feeling overwhelmed with anger and confusion. *A nice little family.* The words rang in his head, but the voice saying them was cynical and disparaging. Connor was appalled. That couldn't have been him!

He glanced quickly from tiny Sarah sleeping in her crib to Courtney, who was trembling in his arms, her face buried in his chest hidden from his view. He loved them! He was so lucky to have them.

Yet he couldn't shake off the memory of a detached and cynical Connor McKay who lived a superficial, self-involved life, who lived for the moment with no thought of the future, who wanted to enjoy the company of women but not a commitment to a woman.

Had that been him before he met and married Courtney? He didn't let himself think that he had been that way as a husband, that he had been hostile and aloof. That he had cheated on her? Was it possible that their marriage was not the happy one he'd lived this past week?

He felt chilled to his very soul. "I love you, Courtney," he said hoarsely, gazing down into her enormous dark eyes.

Courtney felt like crying. "Connor, right now you may think you do but—"

He placed his fingers over her lips. So he was right. There had been something wrong before the accident, something that made her doubt that he would be saying those words if it hadn't occurred. "I know I do," he said fiercely. "Courtney, the reality is *now*. What's past is past, and I'm beginning to think it's best forgotten, after all. What's real is what we have now— you and Sarah and me. Our family."

The intensity of his words, of his hot green gaze, made her weak. Her love for him made her weak. She loved him and wanted him, she wanted to please him, to give and give to him, all of her and all her love. Courtney knew when he scooped her up in his arms and carried her out of the baby's room into their own, that she was going to make love with him.

Caution and control, those two safeguards with which she used to rule her life, to avoid risks, were poor substitutes for the fierce emotions surging through her. Weren't there some risks worth taking? *The reality is now*, he'd said. And reality was loving him.

"Sweetheart, believe me," Connor whispered. He set her on her feet beside the bed, his eyes holding hers.

"Oh, Connor, I—I do," she breathed. She had to believe, she so desperately wanted it to be true.

His mouth closed over hers, hard and hungry, and Courtney's lips parted on a soft moan. He thrust his tongue into her mouth, claiming the soft warmth with bold mastery. Courtney shuddered at the jolt of pleasure that streaked through her body and she arched into him, clinging to him, her senses reeling with the taste, the scent, the feel of him.

They kissed and kissed, hotly, deeply, until both were burning with a searing, primal urgency.

Sometime during those wild, tempestuous kisses, her blouse had become unbuttoned, but Courtney wasn't aware of it until she felt Connor's big hand cup her bare breast. She was soft and warm and lush, and his fingers fondled the satiny flesh, caressing and stroking until she was aching with a pleasure so fierce it almost bordered on pain. He moved his thumb over the taut bud of her nipple and a spasm of erotic electricity jolted through her.

"You're so sensitive, so passionate and responsive," he murmured against her lips. "You're the sexiest, most desirable woman in the world, and you're mine."

He kissed her again, his mouth taking hers with ardent possession. Locked against the long, hard length of his body, she could feel the virile power of his arousal and instinctively rocked against him in an ageless feminine rhythm.

Slowly, he lowered her to the bed, and Courtney was vaguely aware of his hands slipping her blouse from her shoulders and easily discarding her bra as he pushed her back onto the mattress. She opened her eyes to see him staring at her breasts, his eyes filled with desire. And with love.

She forgot to be inhibited, she forgot that this was the first time that a man had ever seen her breasts. Any lingering fear or apprehension that might have been lurking within her was banished. She felt sensual and free, proud to be a woman who was loved and desired by her man.

Connor continued to kiss her, to caress her. He watched her pleasure, her passion build, and satisfaction surged through him. He wanted her to experience a rapture so compelling that the bond between them could never be shaken or broken; he wanted their lovemaking to erase whatever had separated them in the past and bind them together for always.

"I love you, Courtney." His voice was as caressive as his hand, which glided over her stomach and slipped beneath her skirt.

Courtney sucked in her breath as she felt his fingers move seductively along her thighs. His hand smoothed lightly over her panty hose and she felt a shocking urge to feel those hard fingers of his against her bare skin. He kissed her again, his mouth hot and demanding, and she gave in to the voluptuous sensations flooding her. Nothing had ever felt so good—and so absolutely right.

When he lifted his mouth from hers, she stared up at him with love-filled eyes. She caressed his face, the strong line of his jaw and finally the sensual curve of his mouth with her fingertips. "I love you so much, Connor. I—I want you to always remember that, no matter what."

They gazed at each other for a long, quiet moment. Connor felt something intangible yet very real vibrate between them and he realized that this was a profound moment in their relationship, one that neither would ever forget.

He wondered then about other moments, past moments, between them. They were in love and had been married for five years; therefore it stood to reason that they had shared many moments such as these. Then why did he have the strongest feeling that this was the first time they had ever come together this way, in a complete joining of mind, heart and body?

And then Courtney whispered his name and snuggled closer, touching her lips to his, and Connor could think of nothing except how much he wanted her. He took command of the kiss, deepening it, prolonging it, until they simultaneously drew apart, panting and breathless.

Courtney's trembling fingers slipped underneath his shirt, which she had pulled from the waistband of his slacks. She stroked her palm against the hair-roughened warmth of his chest, the material of his shirt confining her, restricting her access. She made a small, frustrated groan.

"We have too many clothes on," Connor said with a husky laugh. "Let's remedy that." He dispensed with her skirt and slip with a few deft movements. Next he skimmed her panty hose down with an expertise that gave Courtney nervous pause. He was very adept at undressing a woman.

"What's the matter, baby?" Connor asked, and she realized that he had been watching her. "Those big gypsy eyes of yours are as round as saucers." And then his eyes narrowed. Gypsy eyes. "Gypsy," he said suddenly. "I used to call you that."

She gulped and nodded. "Is—is your memory coming back?"

"I remember calling you Gypsy." He kissed her lovingly, lingeringly. "I remember how much I love you, how much I want you. Only you, Courtney. Don't ever forget that."

"I won't," Courtney promised fervently. She couldn't. She would remember this beautiful moment forever, no matter what happened. "Connor, I—I'll always remember—"

Her voice trailed off as his fingers slipped audaciously beneath the waistband of her bikini panties. She reflexively parted her legs as his fingers tangled in the soft tight curls between her thighs. Her mind seemed to spin away. What had she been about to say? She didn't know, she couldn't think, she didn't want to. His hand cupped her intimately, his clever fingers making her moan with mindless pleasure.

"Take off your panties while I get undressed," Connor ordered, his voice deep and seductive.

Courtney blushed but obeyed him, her eyes never leaving him as he swiftly divested himself of his clothes. Her mouth went dry at her first sight of a fully aroused nude male. He was so big, so strong, so powerfully masculine. She stared, transfixed, at his muscular chest with the mat of wiry hair covering it, at his abdomen which was flat and hard, and at the dark, dark hair that arrowed lower...

"Come here, darling," Connor said huskily, reaching for her.

They lay down on the bed together, kissing wildly, hungrily, as they touched and stroked and caressed. For a long time the only sounds in the room were soft sighs mingled with deep moans of pleasure.

"I want you now, Courtney," Connor growled. "You're ready for me, sweetheart." He kissed her with rough urgency. "So very ready."

"Yes, Connor, yes!" Courtney whimpered, almost crying from the fierce sensual tension gripping her entire body. His hand was between her legs and she was burning with a delicious pleasure that kept building and building, making her writhe and sob with need.

She watched him settle himself intimately between her thighs. *"You're the sexiest, most desirable woman in the world."* His words echoed in her ears. The look in his eyes made her feel that she really was. And she was his, she belonged to him. She smiled at him, linking her arms around him.

"Courtney." His eyes never left hers as he entered her slowly, carefully, finally filling her with a powerful thrust. "You're so small, so hot and tight," he grated.

Courtney clenched her teeth together. "I'm a little nervous. T-tense." A major understatement if ever there was one, she thought grimly. Connor thought they had been married for five years! If he knew she was a virgin... How could she ever explain it to him? She squeezed her eyes shut to keep the hot tears, which had filled them, from spilling down her cheeks. What if he was furious with her when he learned the truth? What if he hated her and never wanted to see her again?

"I know you're nervous, sweetheart," Connor said soothingly, stroking her cheek with his hand. "Just relax, baby. Relax." He talked softly to her, gently stroking her hair.

Something was going on here, there was something that was eluding him, but his mind was too clouded with passion to work it out. He soothed Courtney instinctively, understanding that she needed him to dispel her fear and tension.

As he talked and caressed and kissed her, Courtney felt her anxiety begin to dissipate. Her body gradually adjusted to his presence. A liquid softness was melting her; she felt sensuously full. She clung to him, savoring the voluptuous, new sensations spiraling through her. And then Connor moved inside her, again and again, deeper and deeper, until she was moving with him and gasping with pure unadulterated pleasure.

She heard herself make a low, sexy sound as she felt herself slipping into some uncharted but sublime oblivion. Their passion flared to a white-hot intensity and they moved as one, becoming one, as their bodies shook with rapturous release, sending them into the realms of ecstasy.

But it wasn't over. They rested awhile, they kissed and talked and teased and played, and then they started all over again.

It wasn't until much later, after their passion had been thoroughly sated, that Connor's mind had cleared enough to enable him to think. Courtney lay sleeping in his arms, her head on his shoulder, one slim leg thrust over his. She was exhausted and replete and had drifted into a deep, relaxed sleep. He was alert and awake, his mind wired, his body energized by the explosive sexual release.

He was flooded with memories that flashed through his mind like pictures in a collage. He remembered other times in other beds with other women. None had come close to what he had shared with Courtney tonight. Never had he felt so close, so connected to anyone, never had he felt so intense and committed and deeply in love.

Which was the way a husband should feel about his wife, of course. There was just one outstanding glitch in their idyllic night of love. Courtney was a virgin. That is, she'd been one until tonight when he had become her first lover. And he was supposed to have been her husband for the past five years!

Connor gazed down at the woman sleeping in his arms. A shaft of moonlight illuminated the delicate features of her face, and her thick, dark hair spilled luxuriantly over the pillow. Somehow, she managed to look both sexy and innocent. Tonight she had been exactly that, a captivating virgin who had been transformed into a passionate lover. By him.

He brushed a soft kiss on the top of her head, feeling protective and possessive. He was her first lover, of that he had no doubt. He was experienced enough to realize her own inexperience and a telltale stain on the sheet added physical proof.

Yet they'd been married for *five years?* And what about the heartbreak of infertility they'd supposedly suffered that had led to the adoption of little Sarah? It went without saying that a woman couldn't get pregnant if she'd never had sex.

And he knew in that moment that they had not been married for five years. He was absolutely certain of it, though memories of their life together still eluded him. But he had one undeniable fact supporting him—that he couldn't have been married to Courtney and not have made love to her until tonight. There was too much passion, too much intensity between them for celibacy to have lasted *five years!*

What if they really weren't married after all? The renegade thought flashed to mind.

Connor immediately rejected it. Courtney and Sarah were his, they belonged to him. He refused to even consider any other possibility. His arms tightened possessively around Courtney as he thought of the past week, all those hours he'd spent with her and the baby. He loved them both, they were a family and they were going to stay a family, no matter what.

Somehow affirming his commitment resolved the

problem. Connor closed his eyes and was soon sleeping as deeply as Courtney.

When the baby's cry pierced the dark silence, Connor sat up at once. His eyes drifted wearily to the bedside clock and he heaved a quiet groan. Four-thirty in the morning!

The baby squalled again. Courtney didn't stir. She was obviously worn out from their vigorous lovemaking. Connor smiled affectionately and kissed her forehead. She'd also been getting up at night with the baby all week. She deserved to sleep.

Slipping from under the covers, he shrugged into his robe and padded into the baby's room. A small night-light lit a path to the crib. Sarah's tiny fists were clenched and her legs were drawn up as her whole body jerked with the fury of her cries. She was hungry or wet or both, and she was letting the world know that she expected the situation to be rectified immediately.

Connor picked her up and carried her to the changing table. Though he usually left diaper detail to Courtney, he had changed the baby a few times this past week, so he knew what he was doing. Sarah stopped crying and looked at him with those wide blue eyes of hers.

"Daddy's here," he said softly, lifting her into his arms. He felt protective and paternal. "Daddy will always be here for you."

Sarah was avidly sucking on her little fist, and he knew that meant she was hungry. "Time for breakfast, huh? What kind of schedule are you on, Cookie? Not even marines in boot camp start the day this early."

He warmed the formula in the convenient electric

bottle warmer plugged into the socket above the bureau. Then he sat down in the rocking chair, the baby and bottle in hand. Sarah made a funny little noise as her small mouth closed over the nipple. Then she was sucking vigorously, staring intensely into Connor's face.

"You're my little girl," he said, his voice soft yet fierce in intensity. "I'm not exactly sure what's going on here, but everything is going to work out for us, Cookie. I promise."

He heard Courtney call his name, softly at first. And then her voice rose in panic. "Connor, where are you?"

"I'm in the baby's room."

Courtney appeared, naked and tousled, to stand in the threshold. "I—I thought you were gone," she whispered hoarsely.

He extended a hand to her. "Come here."

"I'm not dressed." Blushing, she quickly retrieved the demure pink-and-white nightgown that she hadn't had a chance to put on that night. It was ankle-length with a round collar, long sleeves and a ribboned yoke. When she entered Sarah's room wearing it, Connor smiled.

"You look like a virgin straight out of a girls' convent school," he said dryly. It was an ideal lead-in, if she felt like confessing to anything....

Courtney's mouth went dry. "I'm certainly not that," she said quickly, trying to match the lightness of his tone. She thought of the way they'd made love earlier, the erotic abandon, the scorching climaxes, and went hot all over. She'd responded to him in a way she had never dreamed her virginal, inhibited self ever could.

And when she had awakened and found him gone from the bed, she had felt the world crashing down on her. Connor had realized she'd been a virgin, her mind had screamed, he knew they weren't married. He felt trapped in that cage of commitment he so dreaded and was gone for good.

Courtney shivered, remembering. Thank heavens that was a nightmare that hadn't come true. Yet. What was she going to do if it did?

"Come here and sit on my lap," Connor commanded.

She gave a nervous little laugh. "It's already occupied. I won't fit." But she walked over to the rocking chair where he was sitting with Sarah.

With one hand he pulled her down on his lap, then readjusted the baby so that his arms were encircling both. "I'm not going anywhere, Courtney," he said, addressing her earlier fear.

She snuggled closer, curling up in his lap while cuddling the baby in her arms. She had never felt safer or more content, and she wanted to savor the security of the moment.

"Why are you afraid that I'll leave you?" he asked.

Courtney tensed at the question. "I've never been good at goodbyes," she hedged. "All those years Dad was in the army and we had to keep moving, all the people and places we had to say goodbye to...I was heartbroken every time."

But she knew that nothing could compare to the pain she would feel if Connor left—and he would, she reminded herself harshly. Unless, by some miracle, he didn't regain his memory along with his horror of marriage, family and commitment.

She wasn't going to tell him the truth, Connor realized. For some reason—fear?—she wouldn't tell him why she'd claimed to have been married to him for five years, why she'd remained a virgin until tonight, or why they had told Wilson Nollier those tales about infertility preventing them from conceiving a child.

Which brought him to another important point. That claim of infertility was patently false. And he hadn't used any birth control tonight. Unless she had—and he had a very strong feeling that was not the case— he might have made her pregnant.

He gazed down at Courtney, whose head was resting comfortably in the curve of his shoulder, at little Sarah, whose eyelids were drooping sleepily. Another baby?

He found the prospect immensely appealing.

"There aren't going to be any goodbyes," he said, his voice husky and gruffly tender. "You're mine and I'll never let you go."

His mouth covered hers, and his kiss was deep and long and slow, a kiss of possession and commitment. They drew apart reluctantly when the baby stirred.

"I'll put her back in her crib," Courtney said breathlessly, standing up with Sarah in her arms.

He walked her over to the crib, his arm around her. They smiled at each other as Sarah fell into a satisfied sleep almost immediately.

"She is a very accommodating baby," Connor remarked.

"Not always. A few nights ago, she wanted to stay awake and socialize after this feeding." Courtney grinned at the memory. "I could hardly keep my eyes open, but she was raring to go."

"What about now?" Connor swept her up in his

arms and carried her back to their bedroom.
"Sleepy?"

He posed the question as he slipped the girlish
nightgown over her head. She stood naked before him,
feeling sexy and excited and aroused and more wide
awake than she'd ever been in her life.

"No," she replied, standing on tiptoe and winding
her arms around his neck. She smiled into his eyes.
"What do you have in mind?"

Connor laughed lustily. "Maybe a little petting."
He cupped her breasts with his palms, fondling and
stroking the soft rounded warmth, his finger teasing
the taut peaks. "Above the waist."

A breathless little moan escaped from her throat.

"And below," he added sexily, running his hands
over the naked curve of her waist and lower to her
hips. His fingers sunk into the lush softness of her
bottom, squeezing and kneading and exploring the
cleft between.

Courtney whimpered. He pulled her down onto the
bed on top of him.

"I thought we'd do some kissing, too," he continued, and his mouth possessed hers, hot and hard and
deep.

Courtney wrapped her arms and legs around him
and kissed him back, totally surrendering to the fierce
demands of his mouth and his body. When he rolled
her over to her back and thrust into her, she arched
and moaned and clung to him. She wanted him,
wanted him desperately.

"This is what I had in mind, sweet baby," he whispered in her ear, withdrawing himself from her until
he was poised just out of reach.

"Don't leave me," Courtney begged softly. Her fingers clenched him tightly, pulling him to her.

"Never." He surged into her and their bodies merged once more. He whispered words of love, and dark, sexy words of passion to her, and in response, she said things she never thought she would say, things that excited and delighted him.

They moved together as the exquisite pulsing tension built to exhilarating heights, and Courtney held him tight, loving him, as his body shook with sensual tremors that rippled hotly through her. And then his love poured into her and she felt warm waves of almost unbearable pleasure sweeping through her as she climaxed beneath him, crying his name.

Ten

The morning was sunny and particularly warm for April, perfect for walking along Maple Street's tree-lined sidewalks. Courtney and Connor borrowed Mrs. Mason's big, old-fashioned pram to wheel Sarah, who was snugly wrapped and sleeping soundly during her outing.

"It's almost ten," Connor remarked, glancing at his watch. "We should get back. Wilson and—my father should be arriving."

Courtney flinched. She couldn't shake her visceral anxiety that Richard Tremaine's impending visit portended doom for all of them. Suppose Tremaine was as slick and manipulative as his old pal Nollier? Wasn't there some truth to the old "birds of a feather" adage?

For all his wealth and success in the business world, Richard Tremaine's character certainly seemed less than sterling—an adulterous affair, an out-of-wedlock child he had paid a couple to take. And what a couple he had chosen—the unhappily married McKays, from Connor's description, a gambler and his dour wife!

She was miserably certain that it was Connor's amnesia that had inspired Tremaine to seek out his abandoned son after all these years. How could she let an unsuspecting Connor meet this man knowing nothing of the past? Suppose Tremaine, inspired by some sadistic whim, indulged in lies and mind games that Connor was totally unprepared to handle?

"Connor, there is something you have to know," she began, but he immediately cut her off.

"Honey, I know you don't approve of my father visiting me. But—"

"Connor, you don't know him, you never have," she blurted out. "He's simply your biological father, he never married your mother. You don't even know who she is, you were raised by another couple. This morning will be the first time you and Richard Tremaine have ever met. You grew up with Dennis McKay as your father and—and he died six months ago."

She waited for him to register shock, disappointment—*something!*

Instead, he remained calm and collected, in striking contrast to her own agitation. "Courtney, I appreciate your concern, but I see no harm in meeting Richard Tremaine." There was no tension, no hostility radiating from him as there had been in the past when he had discussed the man who had paid to be rid of him. He shrugged. "I think this is a meeting that is probably long overdue."

He picked up his pace, pushing the baby carriage toward Mrs. Mason's house. Courtney dragged behind until he stopped and waited for her to catch up to him. He put his arm around her, pulling her close. "There's nothing for you to worry about, sweetheart."

Nothing? She couldn't shake the unfamiliar but strong urge to burst into tears. Everything was moving so fast; she felt powerless as time and events spun out of her control. Since she'd awakened this morning, she couldn't keep her hands off Connor, couldn't let him out of her sight for a moment. Her body was tingly and aching in places that made her blush just thinking about. She was clingy and dependent, totally unlike her usual strong, spunky self. She loved Connor so much, and she couldn't rid herself of the terrible premonition that she was about to lose him forever.

She nuzzled her face against his chest, holding on tightly to him, never wanting to let go. His hand slid from her waist to her hip, and he spread his fingers wide. "I want you," he said, his voice roughening. "I wish this visit was over and Sarah was napping and we were—" he whispered something so rampantly sexual in her ear that she blushed again.

Her breath quickened and her breasts tightened achingly. Wetness and warmth welled between her thighs. He had such power over her that merely his words could bring her to a state of readiness. She thought of last night's passion and trembled.

She gazed up at him, dazed and shaken. He arched his brows, his smile positively wicked. "I'm remembering, too, Gypsy."

Her heart slammed against her ribs. The way he was looking at her, the way he'd said Gypsy in that teasing, seductive way... Could he possibly—

He bent his head and took her mouth in a hard, swift kiss. Her mind splintered. For the rest of the way back, burning sensual images, memories of his hard body pressing into hers, moving within her, replaced all coherent thought.

Wilson Nollier and Richard Tremaine were already sitting in Mrs. Mason's living room when they arrived at the house. Courtney froze in her tracks at the sight of them.

But not Connor. He calmly lifted Sarah from the carriage and handed her to Courtney before walking toward the two men.

"Connor," Wilson Nollier broke the silence. "This is Richard Tremaine. Your father."

Courtney held her breath. The scene seemed to unfold in slow motion before her eyes. She watched Richard Tremaine extend his hand to Connor, she saw the two men exchange a firm handshake. And then, to her astonishment, Richard Tremaine, the very image of corporate wealth and success with his controlled executive air and impeccable custom-tailored suit, suddenly put his arms around the jeans-clad Connor and hugged him hard.

Her jaw dropped. There were tears in Tremaine's green eyes. Eyes that were so like Connor's in color and shape that she couldn't believe she hadn't realized it the first time she had met him. Of course, she hadn't been aware he was Connor's father then. But Connor had.

She stared, wondering what was going to happen next. She half expected Connor to suddenly announce that he had regained his memory and then berate Richard Tremaine for dumping him on the McKays.

It didn't happen. And while Connor didn't return Tremaine's embrace, he didn't pull away, either.

"My son," the older man said in a voice choked

with emotion. "Connor, I've waited for so long for this day. Thirty-four years. But I never gave up hoping that one day it would occur."

Courtney thought he was laying it on a bit thick and wished that the old acerbic Connor were back to call him on it. She shifted restlessly, watching Tremaine hug Connor again and proclaim his happiness at this long-awaited reunion. Finally she couldn't stand it anymore. "If you were so eager to see Connor, why didn't you contact him before this, Mr. Tremaine?" she asked coolly.

"He desperately wanted to," Wilson Nollier inserted quickly. "But Connor's mother refused to let him have any contact whatsoever with their son. When she married Dennis McKay, she told Richard it was all over between them and that he could never be a part of their son's life. She intended to raise Connor as McKay's natural son. Richard felt he had to respect her wishes. I was astonished to learn that Connor already knew the truth about his father. It's certainly not what Nina planned when she broke it off with Richard. I immediately got in touch with Richard, even before I received word about the accident. He wanted to see Connor right away, but—it seemed prudent to wait a few more days."

"This isn't making any sense." Visibly baffled, Courtney stared at the three men. "Connor said Dennis McKay told him that his mother was Richard Tremaine's girlfriend and that she handed him over to the McKays after Mr. Tremaine paid them a hefty cash settlement to take him off their hands."

"What are you talking about?" snapped Nollier. "His mother never handed him over to anybody. She married Dennis McKay—against my advice, I might add—because she wanted to keep her baby. Thirty-four years ago, a young single woman didn't dare openly raise an illegitimate child on her own. Not that she would've had to. Richard wanted to—''

"So that was the reason why the McKays didn't legally adopt Connor," Courtney cut in, remembering Connor's throwaway remark that day in Kieran Kaufman's office.

"Nina gave birth to her son, she certainly didn't need to adopt him," Nollier said patronizingly. "And in most states, a child born within a marriage is considered to be the legal child of the husband. Certainly in the state of Maryland."

He and Courtney looked at each other, as if realizing at the same time they were the only ones talking. Connor and Richard Tremaine hadn't said a word.

"I never paid anyone to take you, Connor," Richard said, his eyes never leaving his son. "I wanted to be a part of your life, but your mother wouldn't allow it. I sent monthly child support payments directly to Dennis McKay because your mother made it very clear that she wanted nothing from me. She refused to have anything to do with me, she wouldn't even speak to me. I was informed that you believed you were McKay's son and I worried that telling you otherwise would be selfish on my part and traumatic on yours. But I sent the checks to Dennis and he regularly gave me news and pictures of you."

"And Dennis McKay cashed those checks every month and gambled all of it away," Courtney exclaimed indignantly, recalling Connor's cryptic version of his family history. "Connor never knew about or benefited from the money, and I'm sure Mrs. McKay didn't either. She had to work hard to support the family all those years while that—that sociopath wasted Connor's money and then lied to him about his parents!''

She was outraged at the duplicity. Connor had been cheated and his mind poisoned from the time he was a child. The knowledge inflamed her.

''I always suspected that Dennis McKay was a first-class louse,'' Nollier inserted, equally incensed. ''I tried to warn Nina, but she was so damn stubborn. She wouldn't listen to me, she said McKay had agreed to marry her and accept the baby as his own. She wouldn't let Richard go ahead with his plans for a divorce, she insisted he stick with his wife Marnie and—''

''Nina was sick with guilt over our affair,'' Richard inserted quietly. He gazed intently at Connor. ''You see, I was married when I met your mother—''

''But it wasn't one of those sleazy pickups,'' Nollier interrupted with his usual self-righteous ebullience. ''I was with your father the day he met your mother, Connor. Richard had cut his hand at the club and needed stitches. I drove him to the hospital where your mother was a nurse on duty in the emergency ward. They took one look at each other and bam! You know those old movies where fireworks go off when the couple meets? That's what it was like, Connor, I swear. They couldn't fight it, they just fell madly in love.''

''I see,'' Connor said dryly.

Courtney watched him, her anxiety building. He was completely calm and seemed to be taking this awfully well. But then his mind was free of the embittered memories planted and nurtured by the late Dennis McKay. *She* was more emotionally affected by this revisionist version of his personal history than he was.

"Bam, fireworks," she repeated, rolling her eyes heavenward. The old movie imagery was clichéd but rather novel when used as a defense. She responded in kind. "One of those 'bigger than the both of us' kind of things, hmm?"

"It was exactly that, but it didn't justify me cheating on my wife," Richard Tremaine said sadly. "I was dishonest and wrong and I've paid the price for it every day since. I hurt Nina, and in the end I lost both her and my son."

It was his unmistakable sorrow that touched Courtney. She'd been expecting arrogance and rationalization, not genuine remorse.

"Richard, don't be so hard on yourself," Wilson Nollier exclaimed. "Let me paint the full picture for these kids. You were trapped in an unhappy marriage. Your wife didn't understand you."

Courtney frowned. Richard Tremaine might not have resorted to the standard rationalization, but Wilson Nollier had jumped right in with it. Or was this all a carefully orchestrated act, sort of good-cop, bad-cop routine for some elusive, nefarious purpose?

She cast a covert glance at Connor and found him watching her. He moved away from his father to stand by her side. "Why don't you take the baby upstairs and put her to bed?" he suggested quietly. "Then lie down yourself." He gently traced the pale purplish shadows under her eyes with his thumb. "You're tired, you need a nap." He lowered his voice. "You didn't get much sleep last night."

Courtney quivered. It was unfair for him to bring

up last night when she was trying so hard to keep her wits about her to stay ahead of Nollier and Tremaine.

He smiled a lazy, sexy smile that promised...lazy sex. Long, slow loving like they'd enjoyed this morning before getting up. She thought of the drowsy intimacy, the lingering caresses and slow, deep strokes. The exploding pleasure and warm afterglow.

"I'll be up to join you shortly," he promised, watching the pink flush suffuse her cheeks. He smiled.

But if passion had fogged her brain, it hadn't left her totally witless. "You want me out of the way while you talk to—him." She glanced bleakly at Richard Tremaine. He met her gaze steadily, but his expression was enigmatic, giving nothing away.

She was afraid of him, Courtney realized. Tremaine was a wealthy, powerful man with all sorts of connections, with friends in high places. And one of his friends was Wilson Nollier, the unscrupulous baby-seller whom she and Connor had set out to expose. The fact that Nollier had been wonderful to both her and Connor during their time in Shadyside Falls somehow made it harder, not easier, to trust Richard Tremaine.

"Go on up, baby." With his arm around her, Connor firmly walked her out of the room. He dropped a quick kiss on the top of her head. "And stop worrying. Didn't I promise that everything is going to be all right?"

Even then, she might have insisted on remaining, except Sarah's blue eyes suddenly snapped open and her face screwed up as if to wail.

"Uh-oh, her appetite alarm is about to go off," Connor observed, running his finger along the infant's cheek. Sarah reflexively turned her mouth toward it, rooting for a nipple. When she didn't find one, she let out a howl of protest.

Courtney trudged toward the stairs. She had no choice but to leave and tend to the baby. But she was still within earshot when she heard Richard Tremaine say, "Connor, I know you're a lawyer, and I want to offer you your rightful place in Tremaine Incorporated…"

Courtney fairly ran upstairs, a sickening panic setting in. *He thought Connor was a lawyer!* Because she had told Wilson Nollier so, based on the necessity to invent a career that had nothing to do with investigating for *Insight* magazine and the TV tabloids.

Tending to Sarah's needs forced her to focus on the baby rather than the ferocious anxiety that surged through her each time she thought of the quagmire they were caught in. By the time the baby was fed, diapered and put down for a nap, Courtney was calm enough to realize that she needed help.

But not from the usual sources. This wasn't a case for the police or the fire department or any other conventional source of aid. It was an unconventional dilemma that required unconventional assistance. While Sarah slept peacefully in her crib and Connor talked downstairs with his father and Nollier, Courtney dialed the number of the D.C. office of *Insight* magazine.

Kieran Kaufman wasn't at all glad to hear from her. "I have three stories going on here and a deadline that might end up killing me," he barked. "On top of that, my whole life is shot to hell. What do *you* want?"

Courtney swallowed. This wasn't going to be easy. Kaufman was hardly the warm, benevolent type who inspired confidences. Quite the opposite. "Connor has amnesia," she blurted out, even as she was wondering where on earth to start.

Kaufman gave a derisive hoot of laughter. "You've watched one soap opera too many, kid. So what else is going on down there in Shadyside Falls? Do you have a secret evil twin masquerading as you and wreaking havoc all over town?"

"This is serious!" she exclaimed, her voice rising nervously. "Connor thinks he's a lawyer and—"

"He *is* a lawyer," Kieran cut in. "And if you think he has amnesia, you're a world-class nitwit. He's obviously faking it—to get you into bed, maybe? Has it worked?"

Courtney was too shocked to take offense or to make any response at all. Connor really was a lawyer? What he'd said to her on the drive to Shadyside Falls that day came back to her once again: *"What if I were to tell you that I worked my way through college and law school? That I passed the bar exam and am a licensed attorney in Virginia, Maryland and the District of Columbia?"*

Instead of following up on the statement, she'd instantly assumed he was razzing her and had countered with sarcasm of her own.

Kaufman broke the silence. "Anything else? Or do you just want to stay on the line wasting my time?"

"If Connor is a lawyer why isn't he practicing law?" she demanded. "Why is he working as a—"

"I never asked Connor how or why he ended up doing what he does," Kaufman interrupted impatiently. "Hey, I graduated near the top of my class from Columbia's School of Journalism. Why aren't I working at *The New York Times*? Sometimes things work out differently from our original plans."

"Do they ever!" she seconded fervidly. "Kieran, do you—"

"No more of your stupid questions," he interjected rudely. "I gotta go."

"You're certainly in a rotten mood," she snapped before he could hang up on her.

"Yeah, well, it's all your fault. *You're* the one who introduced me to Jarrell Harcourt and screwed up my life."

Courtney was taken aback, first by the abrupt change of subject, and then by the subject itself. "I did not! You introduced yourself to her."

"It's still your fault. If you hadn't been at that club that night, McKay wouldn't have dragged me along and I never would have met her."

"If I remember correctly, you were disgustingly gleeful when you left with her that night. You said she was a, quote, hot new babe, unquote, and thought you were headed straight to the sack." Courtney grinned in spite of herself. "Shall I assume she put a cold, quick end to your delusions?"

"We went to bed that night and we've been together ever since," Kaufman all but wailed. "She says she's in love with me, she wants to marry me! Hell, she might even be pregnant by now. Who can think of precautions when she—when we—" His voice trailed off.

"Clang," murmured Courtney.

"What?"

"Just the sound of the metaphorical cage door slamming shut," she said dryly.

"Damn, I never thought it could happen to me!" Kaufman raved on. "I'm not the type of guy a woman falls in love with—or would even consider marrying!"

"You won't get any argument from me on that. But then I've always thought Jarrell was—well, strange." That was putting it tactfully; the choice of unflattering adjectives that could be truthfully used to describe Jarrell Harcourt was almost unlimited.

"You might not want to admit it, but you're hooked, Kaufman," declared Courtney. "You're in love with her. If you weren't, you would've dumped her the moment she began uttering terrorizing words like love and marriage. I hope you'll invite me to the wedding," she added with malicious glee.

Kaufman snarled a blistering curse and slammed down the receiver so forcefully that the noise reverberated in her ears. Kieran Kaufman and Jarrell Harcourt? Courtney's smile widened. What a perfectly dreadful couple! She wished that Connor had his full memory back so they could share the humor of it together.

She abruptly sobered. When Connor regained his memory, he wouldn't want to share anything with her. He would be furious with her, he would accuse her of manipulating him, of taking advantage of him, of trapping him. Her eyes filled with tears. She had done all those things, hadn't she? And she had the terrible feeling that her reasons—that she'd been afraid and distraught and most importantly of all, that she loved him—would never excuse her in his eyes.

Restlessly she paced the floor, her tormenting thoughts whirling around in her head. She checked on the sleeping baby several times and finally, unable to stand her own company for another second, headed back downstairs.

The living room was empty, and she rushed to the front door, her pulse racing, her imagination immediately conjuring up all sorts of disasters that might account for Connor's absence.

All of which were instantly erased the moment she saw him standing outside at the curb saying goodbye to Richard Tremaine and Wilson Nollier. Relief surged through her, but her heart was still pounding and her limbs felt as limp as overcooked pasta.

Connor came back inside and took a long look at her. "What's wrong sweetheart?" he asked, his voice, his expression, filled with concern.

"You weren't here when I came down." She gave her head a small shake. "I—I guess I was afraid that they'd kidnapped you or something," she said softly, self-mockingly.

"I've already told you I'm not going anywhere." He pulled her close to him, his hands flexing on her waist. "So that precludes kidnapping, doesn't it?"

She leaned into him, clinging to him, wanting to beg him to tell her he would never leave her. He would say it, but she knew the words would provide no reassurance. He'd already said them, and she was positive that they were valid only as long as he believed himself to be her husband.

The moment he learned the true facts...Courtney shivered. He would be gone. "Did the visit go well?" she asked, her voice muffled against his chest.

"Very well, considering the peculiar circumstances," Connor said wryly. "He—Richard Tremaine—my father—offered me a job with the family company. He wants to legally claim me as his son, wants me to meet my brothers and become part of the family."

Courtney's head jerked up and she met his eyes.

"He told me a little about his wife Marnie," Connor continued quietly. "He said she was a sweet, beautiful woman but they never loved each other, that they were too young and bowing to family pressure when they married. It was an advantageous financial alliance for both. Neither were happy, although Marnie had Cole, my older brother, within the first year of their marriage. And then my father met my mother."

"Bam, fireworks," Courtney said softly, quoting Nollier.

"Exactly. He wanted to divorce his wife and marry my mother when she became pregnant, but she wouldn't hear of it. She was certain she was being punished for her sins, and if his marriage broke up, they would both burn in hell forever." He shrugged. "So she chose hell on earth with Dennis McKay, and Richard stayed with his wife and had two more sons. Then Marnie was killed in a car accident. Shortly afterward, Richard went to my mother and begged her to divorce McKay and marry him. She refused."

"More punishment?" Courtney surmised.

Connor sighed. "I guess so. She told Richard that she didn't love Dennis McKay, but she felt she owed him for marrying her and giving me his name, plus she had two other kids by him. She said he was a good-enough father and she couldn't break up her children's home. My father never remarried. He said if he couldn't have my mother, he didn't want anybody else."

"It's sad," Courtney whispered. "Such a waste."

"He said he kept up the fiction of the bereaved widower for his boys, but he wants to tell them the whole truth now." Connor cleared his throat. "He wants to sign over to me a portfolio of stocks and a trust fund that he established years ago in my name. He's going to call my mother tonight and tell her what's going on.''

"Tell her that he's finally claimed you," Courtney said, swallowing hard. "I wonder how she'll take it?"

"I'm more interested in how you'll take it. This will affect all of us, Courtney. You, me, Sarah—and whoever else might come along." He pressed a possessive hand against her belly. Would she at least admit to the hoax of their alleged infertility?

But Courtney, struck by the consequences of Richard Tremaine's call to Connor's mother, didn't make the connection his remark implied. All she could think about was that Nina McKay knew her son wasn't married and wouldn't hesitate to inform Tremaine of that fact.

And then everything would fall apart. She'd been living in a dream world, Courtney acknowledged bleakly. She had been counting on more time to live with Connor and Sarah as a family; she'd thought she had at least until he regained his memory. A hopeful and totally unrealistic part of her had willed that time far into the future.

But now she had only until tonight.

She closed her eyes, resting her forehead against his chest, keeping her face averted to hide her anguish from him. A searing pain ripped through her, so intense that she had to hold her breath to keep from crying aloud. Another parting, another goodbye. She'd lived through so many, but she knew beyond a doubt that this would be the worst of all.

"Is the baby asleep?" Connor asked huskily. He held her closer, arching her into his muscled strength. He nuzzled her jawline, the sensitive hollow below her ear, the slender curve of her neck, breathing in the delicate scent of her skin, tasting it. With a low growl, he covered her breast with his hand, massaging it with slow, sensuous fingers.

The hardening of his body made no secret of what he wanted. He was boldly aroused, pressing hard against her. Courtney released a shuddering breath. The newly awakened, passionate side of her wanted to revel in every sensation coursing through her, to surrender to the moment and to him. To spend these last hours with him making love because it was all she would have after tonight's fateful phone call.

But the defensive coping skills she had developed from years of leave-takings and painful partings reflexively kicked in, eliminating any chances of impulsive passion. Every time the Carey family had received orders to move to another army post, Courtney had managed the pain of separation by withdrawing into herself, by gently but irrevocably detaching herself from those she was about to leave behind.

Automatically she did that now. The news of that phone call was like orders from Uncle Sam.

Just as Connor was about to pick her up and carry her to the bedroom, she pulled herself out of his arms. "It's such a beautiful day," she said, pasting a sunny smile on her face.

Connor did not care to discuss the weather. He reached for her, to yank her back into his arms, but though he was fast, Courtney was even faster. She neatly sidestepped him and crossed the room, her smile growing even brighter.

"I know what we can do today!" she exclaimed with credible enthusiasm. "Go on a picnic! It's a perfect day for it, and the fresh air will be good for Sarah. And for us, too—we've both been cooped up inside that hospital for too long. Mrs. Mason told me about a beautiful park on the edge of town. Shadyside Creek runs through the park, and there is a waterfall there, too. The town took its name from it. Shadyside Falls.''

Connor grimaced. He was as interested in the area's geography as he was in the weather, which was to say, not at all. His body was on fire with a violent need. He wanted her so badly it was all he could do not to stalk across the room, fling her over his shoulder and carry her to bed.

''I don't want to go on a picnic,'' he grated, ''Courtney, I—''

''But Sarah and I do, and we're going,'' Courtney sang out gaily and dashed from the room.

Her departure was so fast and so unexpected that she was gone before Connor had time to act. He heard her talking to Mrs. Mason, who was in the kitchen baking something. The delicious aromas emanating from there didn't tempt him in the slightest.

A picnic? What was going on with her? He narrowed his eyes thoughtfully. She had to have known how much he wanted her. His body had made no secret of that. A thought struck him. Had his blatant desire frightened her? Was her sudden urge to picnic masking an attack of nerves, perhaps the aftermath of last night's passion?

Thinking of last night made him burn with a powerful, ever-increasing, vigorous need. He relived it all—the driving urgency, the feverish heights of pleasure, the fierce, almost primitive urge to mate with her, to indelibly brand her as his.

Had it been too much for her? He broke into a cold sweat at the thought that he might have hurt her. Remembering her responses to him, her soft moans of pleasure, the sweet way she'd clung to him, eased his anxiety somewhat.

Still, she had been a virgin, and maybe she was feeling a little embarrassed and overwhelmed by the passionate demands he had made on her—and by her own on him. Connor frowned. He should've moved faster and hauled her upstairs where he could have swiftly put an end to her post-virginal apprehensions with lovemaking so wantonly intimate and satisfying that she would never again feel inhibited with him.

But she'd caught him unaware, and he had missed his chance. His body pumped with sexual tension that could easily escalate into surging lust with just a modicum of encouragement from her. Maybe if he tried again...

He went into the kitchen and found Mrs. Mason sliding a cookie tray into the oven while Courtney removed several loaves of bread from a tin bread box.

"Connor, how many sandwiches can you eat?" Courtney asked brightly.

She was smiling her social smile, which grated on him because it was the kind of smile she gave to everybody and he'd become accustomed to receiving her special intimate smiles, ones reserved just for him.

"Do you want white, whole wheat or rye bread?" she asked with the impersonal friendliness of a waitress at a lunch counter.

Connor heaved a sigh. It was hardly the offer he'd been hoping for. And with the redoubtable Mrs. Mason firmly entrenched, there was no way he could launch a sensual campaign to make her change her mind.

He breathed a frustrated sigh. "I'm not a fussy eater. Whatever you make will be fine."

So the picnic was on—and he was supposed to turn himself off. He turned and strode from the kitchen, pondering the incredible phenomenon of Connor McKay complying with a woman's wishes.

Eleven

"Admit it, this isn't so bad," Courtney insisted playfully, handing Connor another sandwich. They were both wearing jeans and cotton sweaters, hers yellow and his green, and sitting on a thick faded quilt that Mrs. Mason had loaned them for their outing. The well-maintained park, the pride of the town, was spacious and flat with wooden picnic tables interspersed among the tall shade trees that were already green with new spring leaves. A fast-flowing creek ran through the middle of the park, cascading over a six-foot drop of rocks before continuing its course and eventually emptying into a small tributary of the Potomac River.

Courtney and Connor had chosen to bypass the tables in favor of a shady spot on the ground under the wide branches of a thick-trunked oak tree. Baby Sarah, snug in a portable vinyl carry-bed placed on the far edge of the quilt, seemed completely oblivious to her change of surroundings and slept soundly.

"I know you weren't too eager to come, but you're having fun after all, aren't you, Connor?" Courtney rummaged in the woven straw picnic hamper, also on loan from Mrs. Mason. She pulled out two apples, two oranges, some brownies wrapped in wax paper, a stack of similarly wrapped chocolate chip cookies, a bag of nuts and a bag of candy.

Connor bit into the sandwich—a turkey, ham, cheese, lettuce and tomato combination, his third. "I'll grant you Mrs. Mason packs one helluva picnic basket. This lunch is big enough to feed a Third World country."

"I packed the lunch," Courtney corrected him. "And paid Mrs. Mason for the food, of course."

"Of course. Mrs. Mason sure knows how to turn a buck. Under that sweet, grandmotherly facade is an enterprising 'Have-I-gotta-deal-for-you' entrepreneur."

"What do you mean?" Courtney cast him a swift, apprehensive glance. That remark had sounded startlingly like his old self.

He stretched out his long legs in front of him. "Can't I make a simple comment without it being analyzed and scrutinized? Next you'll be throwing today's date into every other sentence to keep me oriented to time and place like the hospital's well-meaning staff."

Courtney concentrated on unwrapping the brownies and cookies. She offered them to him. "Have some dessert."

Connor arched his brows. "Hoping to sweeten my disposition?"

"Maybe I am. You've been irritable since—"

"You decided that you'd rather have a picnic surrounded by the good citizens of Shadyside Falls—" he extended his arm to indicate the families occupying the picnic tables "—rather than be alone with me."

Courtney's cheeks reddened. Anger, that excellent means of distancing oneself and avoiding pain, swiftly rose within her. "So you're trying to punish me because I wouldn't have sex with you. Instead of enjoying the beautiful day and the lovely park and good food, you're—you're *sulking!*"

"If I am, at least I'm behaving honestly. That cheerful ingenuous act you're putting on is as phony as—" He abruptly stopped speaking and clamped his lips together, as if to physically prevent himself from saying the words he'd been about to say.

As phony as our marriage? The words pounded silently through Courtney's head. Though he didn't know it, it was a heartbreakingly apt comparison. But a fleeting one, for their phony marriage had only a few more hours left.

She scrambled to her knees and started loading the food back into the basket. "I shouldn't have slept with you last night," she muttered, angry at herself, at him and at the cruelty of fate for tantalizing her with what might have been and then capriciously yanking it away. "We got along beautifully all last week, we never exchanged a cross word, but the moment sex was involved—"

"Present tense, Gypsy." He knelt up, bringing himself within inches of her. "Sex *is* involved, very much so." He seized both her wrists and carried her hands to his chest. Automatically she lay her palms against the soft thickness of his sweater, her fingers flexing slightly.

His eyes searched the dark, velvety depths of hers. "You're mine," he said in a fierce, husky whisper. "I'm not going to let you go, and I'm not going to let you push me away."

His thumb traced the shape of her lips, which trembled and parted for him. One big hand slid to the small of her back, and he caressed the sensitive spot until she exhaled a shuddering breath of arousal. He moved his knees apart to widen his stance and drew her even closer to him, nestling her body into his.

Courtney felt the force of his arousal pressing against the most feminine, vulnerable part of her, making her feel full and hot and moist there. When he rubbed intimately against her, her head began to spin. "Connor," she whimpered breathlessly as his mouth descended on hers.

"I know, baby, I know." He slipped his hands under her sweater, gliding them over the smooth bare skin of her back as he sent his tongue deep into her mouth. He kissed her, a deep drugging kiss that she returned in full, giving into all the love and passion she felt for him.

He moved his hands, which were still under her sweater, around her sides and upward to her breasts. "Let's get out of here," he rasped urgently against her ear. "I want to be alone with you. I want to show you how much—how good—" Words failed him and he buried his lips against the soft curve of her neck.

A small breeze rustled the branches, and Courtney felt its cooling effects on her flushed face. With it came a measure of sanity. When she felt his fingers deftly reach for the clasp of her bra, she dug her fin-

gers into his forearms and pushed his hands away.
"Connor, we're right in the middle of the park!" Her
voice was husky and thick, and he smiled at the sound
of it.

"You're right." He moved a few discreet feet away.
"We don't want to shock the picnickers with a scan-
dalizing *public display of affection*. They might be in-
cited to make a citizens' arrest."

He was smiling, his good humor fully restored,
Courtney noted thoughtfully. He'd been as grouchy as
a bad-tempered grizzly when he'd been denied sex,
but now that he thought it was imminent, based on her
undisguised, unreserved response, his mood was as
sunny as the afternoon sky. She suspected she'd just
learned an age-old lesson about men, one that had
been enacted between husbands and wives down
through the centuries.

She felt experienced and sophisticated and wise—
for about a minute and a half. Then reality, in the form
of depression, set in. She was not a wife, and tonight,
after Richard Tremaine informed Connor of their bogus marriage, any chance she might've ever had of
legally becoming Connor's wife would be gone in the
wake of the deception. Her heart aching, she carried
the picnic basket to the car, following in Connor's
wake. She watched him carefully remove little Sarah
from the small bed he was carrying and secure her
into the molded plastic safety seat in the front seat
between them.

Courtney's eyes filled with tears. Connor was so
good to Sarah, so loving and conscientious. The baby
needed him as her daddy as much as she needed him
as her husband. They were a family! But after tonight...

Sarah! Courtney's heart suddenly jumped into her throat, and a wave of anxiety, nauseating in its intensity, crashed over her. Until this moment, she'd been operating under the assumption that Sarah would remain hers, even when Connor left. Now it occurred to her that Richard Tremaine's third call, after the first one to Nina McKay and the second to Connor, would be to his old pal Wilson Nollier.

Of course Tremaine would tell the attorney that there was no marriage. Courtney's breath seemed trapped in her chest, making both inhaling and exhaling nearly impossible feats. She saw two scenarios unfolding after that fateful call. In the first one, Connor kept Sarah as a single father; in the other, the baby was given to somebody else so that he could begin his exciting new life as a Tremaine unencumbered by the constant demands of a child. Neither outcome included Courtney; both were intolerable to her.

She was so preoccupied on the brief drive back to Mrs. Mason's house that she didn't speak a single word. Connor was equally quiet, seemingly lost in his own thoughts. And by the pleased smile on his face and the way his green eyes flicked sexily over her, his thoughts involved an immediate trip to the bedroom, she noted grimly.

If only it could be that easy and uncomplicated, Courtney railed inwardly. If only they really were married and heading home to passionately make love. But they weren't, and wishing, no matter how fervently, wouldn't make it so.

She couldn't have Connor. Though she hadn't accepted the fact emotionally, she had absorbed it intellectually. It was the way her mind had worked from the time she'd been a child, then a teenager during her army-brat years, the way she'd handled separations from best friends and beloved teachers and youthful crushes. Her head knew it was over long before her heart had adjusted to the painful reality.

And her head was telling her it was time to move on and get out of Shadyside Falls, even though her heart was breaking at the thought of leaving.

Courtney glanced down at the baby, sleeping comfortably in the rear-facing car seat. Chances were good that Sarah would sleep another several hours before awakening and demanding to be fed. The fully-stocked canvas bag was in the back seat, crammed with diapers, creams, bottles of formula, flannel blankets and two complete changes of clothes. She had learned from their daily visits to the hospital that one packed for an outing with a baby the way an adult packed for a weekend trip.

She fiddled with the zipper on her purse which lay in her lap. In it, she had money, credit cards, everything she needed for departure. Of course, her clothes and suitcases were still in Mrs. Mason's house, but the landlady could forward them, provided she was adequately compensated for her trouble, of course.

This was it, then. A wave of profound sadness swept over Courtney, and her heart seemed to turn to stone in her chest. There was no use prolonging the agony of goodbye, especially when doing so could cost her Sarah. The maternal bond she'd formed with the baby was unbreakable; she could never give her up.

And Connor? Courtney choked back what felt like a lump of ground glass that had lodged in her throat. She didn't want to give him up, either, but the choice was not hers to make. He was a Tremaine now, out of her reach, and in just a few hours he would learn the truth about their duplicitous marriage. She didn't dare risk the cataclysm that revelation would engender, not with Sarah's welfare at stake. Courtney admitted without shame that if it weren't for the baby, she would gladly cast aside all pride and beg Connor to let her stay with him under any terms he cared to dictate.

But a mother makes sacrifices for her child, a mother places her child's interests above her own—and she was Sarah's mother. She had to remove her baby from the threat of Wilson Nollier and the power of Richard Tremaine.

And that meant leaving Connor. Now.

Connor braked the rented car to a stop in front of Mrs. Mason's house. "I'll keep the key in my purse so we don't lose it," Courtney said, reaching to remove the key from the ignition.

Connor, hot and primed and ready to take her upstairs to finish what they'd started in the park, failed to notice the nervous quaver in her voice or her ghastly forced smile. He got out of the car and walked around it, intending to open the door for her and to carry the baby, still sleeping in the safety seat, into the house.

Before he could reach the door, Courtney hopped over the bulky car seat and took her place behind the wheel. Inserting the key in the ignition, she gunned the engine and took off, peeling away from the curb, tires screeching.

She had a quick glimpse of Connor, standing on the sidewalk, a look of pure astonishment on his face. She didn't dare let herself imagine what he must be thinking. He would be hurt and baffled and upset—at least until he heard from Richard Tremaine.

And then he would hate her. Courtney swallowed

the sob that welled up in her throat and blinked back
the hot tears that burned her eyes. She didn't dare
allow herself the luxury of crying. After all, there was
a child in the car for whom she was completely re-
sponsible. She had to drive, and driving meant keeping
alert and emotionally in control, even though her heart
felt as if it had been shattered into a million pieces.

The road sign indicated the turnoff for Washington,
D.C., and Courtney was about to pull into the exit lane
when she felt a chilling premonition of danger. If Connor had contacted Tremaine or Nollier, one or both
might be waiting at her apartment building for her.
Nollier knew she worked for NPB. A phone call to
the office might yield her address. Her co-workers
were trusting and accommodating and probably would
respond to a plausible reason or request for the information. She didn't dare take the chance.

Courtney glanced down at Sarah, who, blessedly,
was taking an extra-long nap today. Where could they
go? Mark and Marianne lived in nearby Baltimore, but
both Connor and Nollier knew about them and might
trace her there. There was another, more poignant reason why she couldn't seek refuge with her brother and
sister-in-law, Courtney admitted sadly. She wasn't
quite ready to face them with her baby, not after their
fruitless years'-long quest for a child of their own.

She mentally ran down a list of possibilities, eliminating all friends, because this was a predicament that
one should inflict only on family. Moving so often had
strengthened her concept that friends were a temporary
luxury, while family was permanently stuck with you
no matter what.

Her parents were far away in southern Florida, and

her stepbrothers, career army officers, were currently stationed overseas with their families. If they had to stay on the run, she and Sarah might eventually land on their doorsteps, but all were out for the immediate present. Stepsister Cathy lived on the West Coast with her family, so the same applied to her.

That left her sister Ashlinn, in New York City, and her stepsister Michelle, in Harrisburg. Both were within driving distance, both lived alone in their own apartments.

But there was really no decision to make between those two. If she were to arrive at cool, sophisticated Ashlinn's door with a baby and a story about a faux marriage, amnesia, and a long-lost father and son reunion, Ashlinn would probably try to have her committed to the nearest mental institution.

Courtney headed for Harrisburg. Ashlinn might be her full-blooded sister, but she'd always been closer to sweet, understanding Michelle.

Sarah awakened as they approached the city limits and began to fret. By the time Courtney pulled the car into the parking lot adjacent to Michelle's apartment building, the baby was squalling with infant fury.

"It's all right, sweetheart," Courtney soothed, carrying Sarah and the weighty diaper bag up the two flights of stairs to Michelle's apartment. The building had an elevator, but Courtney wasn't about to waste a second waiting for it. "Just one more minute till your dinner, Cookie."

Connor's nickname for the baby came naturally to her lips and brought a swift rush of tears. Standing in the hallway of the building, holding the wailing infant, Courtney had never felt so lost and alone. She missed

Connor with an intensity that bordered on actual physical pain.

She pressed the doorbell, once, twice, three times, without response, then began to think of making alternate plans if Michelle was out for the evening. Just as she punched the bell one final time, the door swung open.

"Michelle, thank God you're here!" Courtney cried, pushing her way inside. And then she gasped.

Michelle hadn't opened the door, a man had. He stood staring at her and the crying baby with a look of incredulity, similar to the one Courtney was giving him.

"Who are you?" Courtney was too disconcerted by the sight of the stranger to manage a polite social greeting. Her dark eyes swept critically over the man, whose shirt was unbuttoned and untucked from the waistband of his trousers, who was barefoot, and who was so stunningly good-looking that she was instantly wary of him.

"I'm Steve Saraceni, a friend of Michelle's." The handsome stranger smiled, doubling, tripling, his attraction. "And I know who you are. You're Courtney, Michelle's sister. I've seen your picture around here."

So he was friendly and charming as well as drop-dead gorgeous? Courtney frowned. "Where's Michelle?" she demanded.

"She'll join us in a moment," Steve Saraceni said smoothly. "Here, let me take your bag." He quickly divested her of the heavy diaper bag, enabling Courtney to shift the baby to a more comfortable position. But Sarah continued to howl.

"She's hungry and needs to be changed," said

Courtney, laying the baby down on a section of the U-shaped sofa.

"How old is she? A couple weeks?" Steve asked affably, watching her tend to the baby. "My sister has a four-month-old son," he added. "I remember his newborn days quite well."

"Courtney!" Michelle rushed into the room, her hair tousled, her pink silk blouse and fashionable pleated slacks so obviously swiftly thrown on, that Courtney winced. Her timing was the worst! Her arrival had clearly interrupted—something.

"Michelle, I'm sorry for barging in like this—"

"A baby?" Michelle interrupted. Her wide china blue eyes swept over Sarah with definite dismay. "Courtney, did you get that baby for Mark and Marianne from the crooked lawyer you told me about? Oh, this is just unbelievable! You've been away and out of touch. Of course, you couldn't have heard the news."

"What news?" asked Courtney. She was stalling for time, not quite ready to tell Michelle that Sarah was completely hers. She cuddled the baby in her arms, giving her a fresh bottle of infant formula.

"The news about Mark and Marianne and the children they've adopted," explained Michelle, sitting down on the sofa. "They received a call from the adoption agency last week, just after you left the city."

Though she was talking to Courtney, Michelle's eyes remained riveted on Steve Saraceni, who was casually straightening and readjusting his clothing. "Three children—a four-year-old girl and two little boys, ages three and one, brothers and sister, were orphaned in a car accident last month. The agency wanted to place the children together, and Mark and

Marianne immediately said they'd take all three. They're picking them up the day after tomorrow.''

Courtney gasped with surprised pleasure. "So they have their family at last! I know they'll make wonderful parents for those poor little kids, Michelle.'' She smiled tremulously. "I—I'm so happy for them I could cry.''

And then she did begin to cry, rocking Sarah in her arms as the tears streamed down her cheeks. What might have begun as a joyfully tearful response to the good news swiftly changed into tears of longing and grief for her own loss. Michelle tried to comfort her, alternating soothing platitudes with tactful questions pertaining to Sarah.

Steve Saraceni disappeared from the room, returning a short time later, fully dressed and impeccably groomed. "Michelle, I can see that you have your hands full here,'' he said in that silky-soft tone of his. "Your sister needs you, so I'll just say goodbye and—''

"No, wait! Please don't go, Steve!'' Michelle jumped to her feet.

Her desperation, so palpable, so totally undisguised, jarred Courtney from the depths of her own misery. Her heart went out to her stepsister, whose eyes were shining with love for this man whose eagerness to go was a unequivocable as Michelle's desire to have him stay.

Oh, Michelle, when it's time to leave, all you can do is let go, Courtney urged silently, bleakly. She'd learned that bitterly hard lesson once again this afternoon.

"None of us has had dinner yet,'' Michelle contin-

ued breathlessly. "I have a whole pan of chicken en-
chiladas in the freezer. I can—"

The sudden insistent sound of the doorbell interrupted her.

"I'll answer it," Steve said quickly.

Courtney half expected him to bolt out the door the
moment he opened it. But he didn't, for the doorway
was blocked by two men, the older in a navy pinstripe
suit, the younger in jeans and a green cotton sweater.

Courtney smothered a cry and began to tremble. No,
it couldn't be! The color drained from her face. She
was so sure she and Sarah could remain safely unde-
tected in Michelle's apartment.

Steve Saraceni's face lit with a beautific smile.
"Why, you're Richard Tremaine!" he exclaimed, addressing the older man. "I recognize you from your
pictures on the financial pages," he added reverently,
thrusting out his hand to shake. "I'm Steve Saraceni.
Terribly pleased to meet you." He turned to face
Michelle, his handsome face aglow with admiration.
"Darling, I didn't know you knew Richard Tremaine."

Michelle stared from Steve to Courtney to the two
men standing in the doorway. "I don't," she said be-
wilderedly.

Connor stepped forward, into the apartment. His
eyes locked with Courtney's, and she swiftly looked
away, gazing fixedly at Sarah in her arms.

"Uh, Richard, why don't you take Michelle and—
Steve here out to dinner while Courtney and I talk,"
Connor said, his voice low and taut with a steely control that made Courtney shiver. Acting instinctively
from a sense of sheer self-preservation, she stood up

and began to slowly inch her way out of the living room.

"Good idea!" Richard Tremaine seconded heartily. "Michelle, Steve, I'm sure you two can recommend a good restaurant."

"Yes, sir, I certainly can." Steve Saraceni was beaming. "Name your choice of cuisine and I'll name the best place for it. Michelle, come, sweet." He extended his hand, and she hesitated for just a moment before taking it.

"What brings you to our fair city, Mr. Tremaine?" Steve asked, turning the full force of his charming smile back to Richard Tremaine. "I hope you are enjoying your—"

The three left the apartment, Saraceni keeping up a steady stream of conversation.

Connor and Courtney were left alone. She continued her subtle progression out of the room, too unnerved by his presence to do anything else.

"Who is that silver-tongued smooth operator sucking up to my father?" Connor asked, moving slowly, purposefully, toward her.

"I—I just met him here a short while ago." Even to herself, Courtney's voice sounded high and unnatural. "I think he's involved with Michelle."

"Michelle may be involved with him, but he is involved only with himself," Connor observed. "I know his type so well I can make an on-the-spot judgment call."

"How did you know I was here?" Courtney whispered, her heart in her throat.

"Because I used to be his type." Connor ignored her question and answered an entirely different one. "And sure, it's cool, it's fun. You're completely free and answer to no one. You avoid obligations and responsibilities. Your money and your time is all your own. And then you find yourself at a certain age, at a certain time, when it all begins to pale. You realize that you have no friends you can really talk to or depend on, that there is no woman you can trust and feel close to. Suddenly not even sex has any real pleasure or meaning. It's become just an exercise, a way to work out and work off tension.''

''Connor,'' Courtney cut in nervously.

''Heard enough of my soul-searching soliloquy, huh?'' He smiled without mirth.

''You remember!'' she exclaimed. Suddenly the pieces fell into place. Some of them, anyway. ''You must have remembered me mentioning Michelle to track me here!''

''Yes.'' He nodded. She could read nothing in his enigmatic expression. ''I remember everything, Gypsy.''

Courtney felt hot, then cold. She didn't understand and she didn't dare to hope. ''When?'' she asked shakily.

''Last night. It happened in stages. First it occurred to me that you couldn't have stayed a virgin if we'd been married for the past five years.''

She winced, and a slow hot blush turned her cheeks crimson.

''But it wasn't until we made love again, after the baby's four-thirty feeding, that it all came back to me. Everything. The adoption story, our marriage ruse to fool Wilson. The only gap in my memory is the time following the collision until I awakened in the hospital.''

''So when we were on our walk this morning and

when you met your father...during our picnic...you remembered everything?" she whispered.

He nodded.

"Why didn't you tell me?" she cried. "I—"

"I tried," he cut in. "Well, sort of," he modified when she gave him a look of pure disbelief. "I told you not to worry and that everything was going to be all right. I said you were mine and I'd never let you go."

"You'd been saying those things before your memory returned," Courtney reminded him. "How was I to know—"

"The truth is, I wasn't quite sure how to tell you or how you would take the news," he interrupted her again, his lips curving into a tight, sardonic smile. "Maybe I was worried that you would get scared and take off."

They were in Michelle's bedroom now. Courtney was shaking so much, she could hardly stand. She stared at the rumpled bed and her blush deepened. Oh, she had interrupted something here, all right. And then Burton, Michelle's Siamese cat, emerged from under the bed, greeted them with a meow and hopped onto the pillows. Courtney stared at the cat, who gazed inscrutably back at her.

"Let's go back into the other room," Connor suggested dryly. "There's too much in this one competing for your attention." He reached for Sarah. "Here, let me take her."

Courtney's eyes filled with tears. "I can't give her up, Connor," she whispered.

He gave her a measuring glance, then took the baby from her arms and carried her into the living room. Courtney followed him, watching as he removed a blanket from the canvas bag and spread it over a sofa cushion. He carefully laid Sarah down on it, tucking a smaller flannel blanket around her.

Then he straightened and turned to face Courtney. "Why did you leave me? No, let me amend that to 'Why did you run out on me?' Because that's exactly what you did, Courtney."

"I had to!" She gulped back a sob. "What was between us wasn't real, and once your father called your mother, it would've been all over, anyway."

"That's the stupidest thing I've ever heard!" His eyes glittered, his tone was fierce. "I told you I loved you, you said you loved me, too. It doesn't get any more real than that."

"But you said it under false pretenses! You thought we were married!"

His face softened. "And you thought I wouldn't want you if I remembered that we weren't?" He moved closer and slid his fingers into the dark silkness of her hair. He lowered his voice. "So the little Gypsy packed up and moved on."

"I had to," she repeated, blinking back the emotional tears that once again welled in her eyes. Her hand reached up and covered his. "Before the accident, the one thing you didn't want was to be married. You insisted that I had to give the baby back to Nollier, and you accused me of trying to trap you—"

"That was before I had some sense knocked into me." He grinned suddenly. "Literally."

"Don't make jokes about it!" Courtney shuddered. "It was awful seeing you lying unconscious in the hospital."

"Which brings us to Dr. Ammon's esoteric concept of disassociative amnesia." Connor used his other arm to haul her against him. "The internal conflict I was waging was over you, baby. You were everything I wanted, everything I needed—"

"Everything you'd spent your adult life avoiding," she finished, staring up at him with enormous dark velvet eyes. His hard, strong body felt so good against hers. She slipped her arms around his waist, daring to allow herself to lean into him.

"I was an idiot, and that car accident was a blessing in disguise because it gave me the chance to know what it was like to be your husband and Sarah's father." His arms tightened around her, his hands soothing and caressing. His lips moved, warm and tender, against her temple, her cheek, the curve of her neck.

"It was pure heaven. Marry me, Gypsy. I want to replace that fake wedding ring with a real one. I want to love you and live with you for the rest of my life." He smiled into her eyes. "I want to laugh with you and fight with you and play games with you and go on stupid picnics with you... Help me out here, Gyps. Give me a yes."

"Yes! Oh yes, Connor." She clung to him, gazing up at him, laughing through tear-blurred eyes. "It's like a wonderful dream coming true! I love you so much. I want to be your wife and raise our children—"

"Which means we'd better get married immediately since we already have our first child." Connor grew serious. "Courtney, we're going to go through the correct channels and make sure that Sarah's adoption is completely legal and aboveboard."

"We won't have to give her up, will we, Connor?" Courtney asked anxiously. "Please, no, not even for a short while."

"Relax, Gypsy, we don't have to." He smiled broadly. "My father already made all the necessary calls and proper arrangements. We have a first class, *ethical* attorney handling the case."

"Which brings us to Wilson Nollier." Courtney grimaced.

"I told my father everything about him, Courtney. He was appalled and called Nollier immediately. From now on Wilson is going to refocus his practice and not handle any more adoptions. Ever. My father has certain 'watchdogs' who will make sure he doesn't."

"So Nollier's racket has ended, after all," Courtney said thoughtfully. "He'll be out of the *Insight* story and the NPB documentary, but he's not working in the adoption field anymore, anyway. Does he hate us?"

"Not at all. Wilson isn't stupid. He knows it's better to be a friend of the Tremaines than an enemy."

"The Tremaines," she echoed softly. "You've finally made your peace with your father, your real father." She held him tight. "I'm glad for you both, Connor."

"I haven't decided if I'll add Tremaine to my name or stick with McKay. Do you have a preference?"

Courtney smiled. "Only that you make the decision yourself and are content with it."

"I am going to accept the position my father offered me with Tremaine Incorporated. If it doesn't work out, I'll work somewhere else—as an attorney," Connor added succinctly.

"Your days as a self-styled, free-wheeling fact-finder are over, hmm?"

"Definitely. I have a wife and a child to provide for." He slipped his hand between them and gently stroked her belly. "Maybe another one as well. I didn't use protection, Gypsy. The first few times I thought we didn't have to."

"And the other few times, when you knew?" she asked provocatively, gazing at him with sexy, flirtatious eyes.

"I wanted to make you pregnant," he admitted boldly. "And I'm going to, Gypsy."

"Do I hear the sound of the metaphorical cage door permanently closing?" She laughed up at him.

"No, sweetie, you have it backward. The door has opened. You set me free from that miserable cage of loneliness and distrust."

"I love you, Connor," she said, gazing at him, her heart in her eyes.

He took her mouth in a passionate kiss, sealing their engagement, marriage and parenthood all at once. There would be no more partings, no more goodbyes. They were inseparable, together forever.

* * * * *

This summer, the legend
continues in Jacobsville

Diana Palmer

A LONG, TALL TEXAN SUMMER

Three **BRAND-NEW** short stories

This summer, Silhouette brings readers a special
collection for Diana Palmer's LONG, TALL TEXANS
fans. Diana has rounded up three **BRAND-NEW**
stories of love Texas-style, all set in Jacobsville,
Texas. Featuring the men you've grown to love from
this wonderful town, this collection is a must-have
for all fans!

They grow 'em tall in the saddle in Texas—and
they've got love and marriage on their minds!

Don't miss this collection of original Long, Tall Texans
stories...available in June at your favorite retail outlet.

Take 4 bestselling love stories FREE

Plus get a FREE surprise gift!

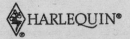

Back by popular demand...

DIANA PALMER's
Long, Tall TEXANS III

They're the best the Lone Star State has to offer—and
they're ready for love, even if they don't know it!
Available for the first time in one special collection,
meet HARDEN, EVAN and DONAVAN.

LONG, TALL TEXANS—the legend continues as
three more of your favorite cowboys are reunited in
this latest roundup!

Available this July wherever
Harlequin and Silhouette books are sold.

HARLEQUIN®   Silhouette®

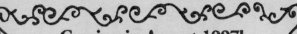

Coming in August 1997!

THE BETTY NEELS
RUBY COLLECTION

August 1997—Stars Through the Mist
September 1997—The Doubtful Marriage
October 1997—The End of the Rainbow
November 1997—Three for a Wedding
December 1997—Roses for Christmas
January 1998—The Hasty Marriage

COLLECTOR'S EDITION

This August start assembling the
Betty Neels Ruby Collection. Six of the
most requested and best-loved titles have
been especially chosen for this collection.
From August 1997 until January 1998,
one title per month will be available to avid
fans. Spot the collection by the lush ruby red
cover with the gold Collector's Edition banner
and your favorite author's name—Betty Neels!

Available in August at your favorite retail outlet.

◆ HARLEQUIN®

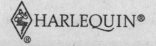